1

Also by Stewart Home, published by The Do-Not Press

*Cunt*

# Down & Out in Shoreditch and Hoxton

## STEWART HOME

THE DO-NOT PRESS

First published in Great Britain in 2004
by The Do-Not Press Ltd
16 The Woodlands, London SE13 6TY

Copyright © Stewart Home 2004

The right of Stewart Home to be identified as the
author of this work has been asserted in accordance
with the Copyright, Designs and Patents Act 1998.

*British Library Cataloguing-in-Publication Data*
A CIP catalogue record for this book is available
from the British Library.

A Paperback Original
ISBN 1-904316-26-3

1 3 5 7 9 10 8 6 4 2

Set in Sabon.
Printed and bound in the United Kingdom

www.thedonotpress.com

For my mother, Julian Callan-Thompson.
Born Newport, south Wales, 7 January, 1944.
Died London, 2 December, 1979.

To begin with transformations. I decided to throw away my own rules. I planned crimes against grammar by immersing myself in the grammar of crime. Around Bishopsgate. North and east. The area was changing. I'd read my Robert Greene. *A Notable Discovery of Cozenage. The Second Part Of Cony-Catching. The Third And Last Part Of Cony-Catching. The Black Book's Messenger. A Disputation.* Greene provided evidence that common prostitutes had plied their trade here for at least 400 years. Now things were changing. Warehouses converted to loft apartments. Kwik Save gone. Hoxton, Shoreditch, Spitalfields, would never be the same.

I wanted to bring back the image of the dell, the doxie, the bawdy basket, to an area that gentrification was trying to sweep clean. The working girls were being hemmed in. It was risky to work the traditional corners. Hanbury and Commercial Streets. The new middle class residents were adept at getting the cops to clamp down on vice, and this a victimless crime.

Strapped in, strapped on, stepping out. I charge extra for sex at Jack The Ripper murder sites. Prostitution documented as one of the fine arts. There were precedents. Crime is the highest form of sensuality.

My economic position was every bit as precarious as any other prostitute. My work as an artist brought in little money. Rents were sky-rocketing in Shoreditch and Hoxton. I'd moved to the Boundary Estate because it was cheap. That wasn't the case any more. I longed for my own council tenancy but had to get by sub-letting. I liked Shoreditch. Unlike Brixton and Hackney, where anarchists rebelling against their middle class backgrounds had been the first to spot the opportunities for cheap and free housing, my area had become desirable thanks to a genuine community feeling among artists.

However, while economic necessity was a motivating factor in my desire to bring traditional bawdy-basketing back onto the streets, other issues were involved too. A lot of ground had been covered by feminist artists in the 1970s. Mary Kelly had explored motherhood, while Cosey Fanni Tutti examined the world of pornography and stripping. The diversity of positions taken by Kelly and Tutti showed the strength of feminism as a movement way back when. I wanted to do more than follow in Tutti's footsteps. I was determined to push back the boundaries with my art. I would document commercial sex.

Just as a philosopher produces ideas and a poet verses, a prostitute produces crime. But if the relationships between this latter branch of production and the edges of society is examined closely, one is forced to abandon a number of prejudices. The prostitute produces not only crime but also the vice laws. She produces the professor who delivers lectures on these laws, and even the inevitable text-book in which the professor casts his lectures onto the market as a commodity. The result is an increase in national wealth, quite apart from the pleasure which is derived from the crime.

Further, prostitution as the oldest criminal profession produces the whole apparatus of the police and criminal justice, bailiffs, judges, jurors etc., and all these different occupations, which constitute so many categories of the social division of labour, develop diverse aspects of the human spirit, create new needs and new ways of satisfying them. Sadism itself has provided occasion for the most ingenious mechanical inventions, employing a host of honest workers in the production of sex toys. The prostitute arms herself with whips, chains and condoms. When arrested she is charged with soliciting, never with being equipped to commit a crime.

The prostitute produces an impression, now moral, now tragic, and renders a service by arousing the moral and aesthetic sentiments of the public. She produces not only text-books on vice, not only law books and thus the legislators, but also art, literature, novels and even tragic drama – the tart with a heart of gold whose carnal nature is her fatal flaw. The prostitute interrupts the monotony and day-to-day security of bourgeois life. She protects it from stagnation and brings forth that restless tension, that nobility of spirit without which the stimulus of competition would itself become blunted.

The prostitute gives a new impulse to productive forces. Prostitution releases from the employment market a portion of excess labour power, diminishes competition amongst workers, and to some extent stops wages falling below the minimum. The war against vice absorbs another part of the same population. The prostitute therefore appears as one of those natural equalising forces which establish a just balance and open up a whole field of related occupations. The influence of the prostitute upon the productive forces can be shown in detail. Call girl scandals sell newspapers. Think of Hugh Grant and Divine Brown. Keeler and Profumo.

I needed a new name. A brassy attitude. I called myself Eve. The punters swallowed it. I swallowed the punters. Mechanical sex and a name that in many countries is associated with the first human crime. I worked in the dark, by instinct. Kerb crawlers and pedestrians. Policemen paid off with a blow job. Lonely men buying friendship and wanting everything both ways. Three way fucking. Half the work and twice money. I planned to be a cripple when I got older. Charging extra for perversions. Less is more. Only three limbs and the price quadruples. Suck my left one.

The men I met often chattered but rarely listened. Several were writers. Take Adam Scald: he was after material for a book. Still, he parted with his cash and wanted the business. Wanna burn rubber or is it french for you, darling? I led him down Wentworth Street to Green Dragon Yard. He wanted full sex between sheets. That cost extra. He shelled out the surcharge. I led him up Brick Lane and onto the Boundary. He was taken aback by my pad. I had too many books for his liking. It shattered his image of me as an innocent.

Adam had problems exploiting a woman of his own

class. A woman who was obviously intelligent. I told him he was being sentimental. I was, however, happy to keep his money if he wanted to leave. Then the cops intervened. City of London. The Old Bill were raiding Michael, the semi-professional burglar who lived across the landing. Adam was impressed and got even more excited when I explained that my estate had been built on the site of a notorious rookery. The Old Nichol. Michael's wife Mandy was swearing on her little boy's life that her husband wasn't in.

Michael was climbing out of a back window. A cop stationed in a van spotted him. Lost him. A radio message to the rozzers dealing with Mandy put them in the picture. The Old Bill were pissed. They called Mandy fat. Shifted to insults predicated on her mixed race relationship. Then it was punishment time. The cops stole all the shoes belonging to Mandy and Michael's ten year-old son. Mandy flipped out. Asa wouldn't be able to go out without shoes on his feet. The Old Bill roared she'd get the nipper's stuff back when Michael handed himself in.

This incident with the cops got Adam all steamed up. I forcefully reminded him that not even a lady of the night wants her clothes ripped by a punter desperate to get them off. Scald's passions were boiling over so I made him lie on the bed. It was time to demonstrate to the over-sexed john that I'd taken command of the situation. I rolled a condom down his length and this was enough to make him come. He was like putty in my hands. No need for penetration. He wasn't up to it once he'd shot his load.

Cheap thrills. Part of a low budget life-style. What interested me was the relationship between quantity and quality. The dividing line between pleasure and pain. My own inability to differentiate between art and crime. Adam wanted to know more. I charged him. He insisted I sit on his face once he coughed up the readies for my discourse. I was amenable. I slipped the notes Scald gave me into my bra, straddled him and got on with my diatribe. Freedom was the crime that contained all other crimes. Only art could cut the umbilical cord linking necessity and freedom.

Mandy, Mandy, you're doing my head in! The cops had fucked off and Michael was back. He was known on our estate as The Moron. He had trouble making friends his own age. When he was about, The Moron spent his days regaling local schoolboys with tall stories about theft and doing time. He was sufficiently socialised to restrict himself to vandalising his own block; he'd never burgled the neighbours. Mandy,

Mandy, you're doing my head in! It was a mantra. Mandy's next social security payment was eight days away. She was volubly demanding money to buy Asa new shoes.

The walls were thin and Scald got his rocks off listening to The Moron squealing that Mandy was doing his head in. Mandy had a humungous gut. The Moron was thin. They fought constantly but the match wasn't even. Unable to externalise his frustrations by punching out his wife. The Moron kept a brick by their front door so that when things got too much for him, he could rush out and smash one of the block's communal windows. When this happened, Scald blurted out that such behaviour made a kitchen sink drama like *Look Back In Anger* appear tame.

Adam was suitably astonished by the denouement to this domestic. Mandy slamming the door on The Moron as he attempted to get back into their flat. The Moron thrust forward at the last moment, breaking four fingers which were caught between the door and the jamb. Since her husband was screaming blue murder, Mandy attempted to make things up with soothing words. The Moron had never really grown up, as was evident from his cussing and crying. Things only quietened down once a taxi arrived to speed the ill-starred couple to accident and emergency at the Royal London Hospital.

I found out later that, after arriving at their destination, my neighbours discovered they didn't have the readies to pay for their ride. The cabbie seemed cool, his boss called the cops. The Moron was arrested while being bandaged up. Once he'd been put away, my block became a considerably more pleasant place. No more teenage boys lurking on the stairwell waiting for The Moron to appear with his tall tales. Of course, things got worse for Asa. Without his dad about he became a soft target for the other kids, who picked on him because he was grossly overweight.

Adam was hooked. He was fascinated by my discourse about quantity transforming itself into quality. Crime became art and art became crime. Scald could see a book. I saw a monograph but not by Scald. He wrote journalese, not art criticism. Besides, there was a danger that he might seek a quick injection of cash from a broadsheet for a feature. That wouldn't do. My project needed time to develop before being bathed in the raw light of media exposure. No problem though. I had a plan that involved a brothel, several whores and a lot of polymorphous sexual stimulation.

Thomas De Quincey's essay 'Murder Considered As

One Of The Fine Arts' first appeared in Blackwood's Magazine in 1827. Although De Quincey is a notoriously tiresome writer, it has long been a diverting pastime to read certain of his passages as if he were a philosopher. De Quincey's horrified description of Wordsworth cutting the pages of a book with a dirty butter knife is an existentialist tour-de-force, more convincingly unreal than his dream and opium passages. Likewise, having studiously adopted a literal reading of the essay on murder, this interpretation has become a matter of conviction for me.

Having by this time drunk the better part of a bottle of Four Roses bourbon, it occurred to me I was vocalising my thoughts when Adam suggested De Quincey's obsession with the prostitute Little Annie was more relevant to my concerns. Scald observed that, like contemporary London novelists such as Iain Sinclair, De Quincey was a psychogeographer in deed if not name. So then, Oxford Street, stony-hearted stepmother, thou that listenest to the sighs of orphans and drinkest the tears of children, at length I was dismissed from thee! I no more pace in anguish thy never-ending terraces.

Adam was declaiming from the *Confessions*: Being myself, at that time of necessity a peripatetic, or walker of the streets, I naturally fell in more frequently with those female peripatetics who are technically called common streetwalkers. Some of these women had occasionally taken my part against watchmen who wished to drive me off the steps of houses where I was sitting; others had protected me against more serious aggressions. But one amongst them – the one on whose account I have at all introduced this subject – yet no! Let me not class thee, noble-minded Ann with that order of women...

Oh youthful benefactress! how often in succeeding years, standing in solitary places, and thinking of thee with grief of heart and perfect love – how often have I wished that, as in ancient times the curse of a father was believed to have a supernatural power, and to pursue its object with a fatal necessity of self-fulfilment, even so the benediction of a heart oppressed with gratitude might have a like prerogative; might have power given it from above to chase, to track, to follow, to haunt, to waylay, to pursue thee into the central darkness of a London brothel.

Talk of a seraglio brought my thoughts back to murder. I needed to cover my tracks, cut off any premature coverage of my art, see to it that Scald died in Pocket-Mouthed Meg's house of ill-repute. The brothel was a backdrop, a hyperreal film set, an exotic location for the perfect crime. Snuff movies had long been the stuff of myth but I'd yet to meet someone who'd actually seen one. I planned to make a snuff movie with a difference. Scald would be the author of his own demise: he was going to be fucked to death.

A climax must necessarily be delayed. Indeed, true pleasure comes from its endless deferral. I called Meg and told her everything was on. At that moment, she was doing a roaring trade. The film would be shot on digital video. The crew would consist of one woman. That wasn't the problem. Set-up was easy, we just had to wait until things were less frantic at the whorehouse. Four, maybe five or six in the morning. Refreshing our drinks I announced that Manet's Olympia was painted in 1863 and images of sexual exploitation had been popular amongst artists ever since.

I was beginning to warm to this theme when Adam asked me about the noise that was coming from the flat above mine. Bhangra music was being pumped at volume through a hi fi system and a bunch of men were engaged in noisy conversations. I had to explain that institutionalised racism meant there were few employment opportunities for local Bangladeshi men outside the catering trade. Knocking off from their restaurant work around midnight, it was only natural that my neighbours would want to socialise for a few hours before going to bed. Adam was horrified by my blasé attitude.

I reassured Scald that the partying wouldn't go on long. It was Ramadan. The men would rise early to say their prayers. I put on Plastikman's *Sheet One*. but my guest didn't like dance music. Adam asked for classics but Varèse went down badly and Cardew was sneered at because he'd provided striking workers with musical entertainment. I had the 'Glenn Gould Edition' of Bach's *The Well-Tempered Clavier*. This CD set – which had been promoted under the banner 'Neither "Teutonic Severity" Nor "Unwarranted Jubilation"' – was not to Scald's liking. He favoured the simplicities of Mozart's reductive drive for tonality.

According to Adam, research conducted at the University of California proved that listening to Mozart boosted your IQ. I insisted measurements of intelligence are culturally determined. You can "prove" almost anything with statistics, and, as far as I was concerned, the generic nature of Mozart's music led to passivity and conformism. Brain tumours were more mind expanding. Scald got upset about the fact that Glenn Gould spliced together various studio recordings into a single piece. This, apparently, was the mark of a faker who lacked virtuoso talents. Naturally enough, I retorted that both genius and the virtuoso were bourgeois constructs.

Adam attacked what he took to be a print of Vladimir Tretchikoff's 'The Chinese Girl' (1952) that hung above my gas fire. I ribbed Scald for his inability to distinguish posters from original works of art. My flat reflected my mind: both were well proportioned occult memory systems filled with stratagems and decoys that drew on the traditions of trompe l'oeil. Scald vainly condemned my tastes as kitsch. His understanding of art was bi-polar rather than dialectical. He was unable to see that, for me, illusionism was simply a mirror in which the world was reflected back on itself.

The Tretchikoff was not a Tretchikoff, it was culled from a series of works in which I'd corrected the modernist "faults" of middle-brow "masters" such as Henry Major and Sir Alfred Munnings. The face, hair and blouse in my painting were carefully modelled on the traditionalism of the "original". But where, under the influence of modern art, Tretchikoff had only outlined the hands and failed to provide a background, I'd added these "missing" details. I wouldn't countenance loose drawing. The flock wallpaper in my painting

'The Chinese Grrrl' (1995) matched the rolls with which I'd decorated my living room.

Every reform – however necessary – will be carried to an excess by weak minds, which will itself need reforming. Adam was unaware that his invocation of Coleridge sounded ambiguous. He admired this romantic poet's conservatism. He followed the epigram with an anecdote concerning heretical religious tracts that was also lifted from the *Biographia Literaria*: It is not easy to imagine anything more fantastic than the very appearance of their pages. Almost every third word is a Latin word with a Germanised ending, the Latin portion being always printed in Roman letters, while in the last syllable the German character is retained.

It didn't seem to have occurred to Adam – or his hero – that English was concocted from a similar fusion of Germanic and Romance languages. Since Coleridge freely mixed his own prose with that of Idealist philosophers such as Schlegel, it's difficult to understand his disdain for practices of this type. Perhaps he lifted the prejudice from Hobbes, who asserted that the authority of the sovereign's law depended upon establishing unambiguous proper meanings for words. Unlike Scald and Coleridge, I wanted to do away with the language of judgement, and this necessarily entailed a revolt against the ossified conventions of crime.

The conversation twisted back to De Quincey. It was difficult to see how 'Murder Considered As One Of The Fine Arts' had acquired the status of a classic. This essay, like so much Romanticism, required an editor who was unafraid to prune it savagely. Indeed, it is a fact that every writer of eminence has either been murdered, or at the least been very near murdered – insomuch that, if a man call himself an author and never had his life attempted, rest assured there is nothing in him; and against De Quincey's work in particular, it is an unanswerable objection.

Adam accused me of having no feeling for great literature. I replied that I enjoyed peace, tranquillity and bourbon. I was drunk. I slurred my words. A lot of whores have booze or drug problems. I was no stucco angel, I'd made myself into a plaster harlot. A streetwalker, prostitute, call girl, bawd, courtesan, strumpet, trollop. I lifted a gartered leg and gave Scald a flash of the minge that I'd barely covered with my mini. Or was it that I'd barely covered my mini with a mingy skirt, a garment short on material? Scald's mickey strained against his fly.

He fumbled with his wallet. I pushed it aside. I'm every man's fantasy, a prostitute who sometimes gives it out for free. Adam dropped his pants. Stood up. His crank was straight and stiff. I sucked the lead-coloured knob as it rolled in and out of my mouth. Scald wriggled rearwards and three quarters of his dial appeared beneath my nose. Then he bore forward so that nearly all of it went between my red lips. I met his movements, bent my head forward in little bobs, clasped his handle with both my hands. Adam came in my face.

My memories are principally visual. I remember images above all. I'm certain that as I sucked Scald's covenant my gasps were accompanied by his groans. That said, I have no recollection of this noise. Adam stumbled back from me, fell to the floor. Swearing, cursing, blaspheming, cussing, imprecating. He called me a slut, bitch, blue girl, doxie, bovine, heifer, stupid tart, perverted, depraved. Since I was obviously a well-educated girl, Scald wanted to know where I'd learnt my lewd, lascivious, lustful, lecherous, licentious ways. Had I been raped by my father, seduced by a libertine, corrupted by a rake?

Since I'd read John Cleland and Kathy Acker too, rather than providing Adam with a straight reply, I gave him Fanny Hill's history filtered through my time at art school. The memoirs of a woman of pleasure. Kathy went to Barnes, Eve found herself in Liverpool. Induction week at art school. Getting-to-know-each-other parties. Cheese and wine. The freshers nervous. Lecherous old tutors eyeing fresh talent. My satyr bore down on me grinning in a way entirely peculiar to himself. His odorous presence confirmed in me the sentiments of detestation to which his mere appearance first produced.

The lecturer sat down beside me. He guzzled wine while ogling my bristols in a manner that caused me both pain and confusion. The freshers I'd been chatting with melted into the party crowd, burdening me with the task of entertaining this lecherous goat. Foolishly, I asked him about his art. He insisted that he couldn't talk about his painting until I'd seen examples of it. My arm was grabbed and I found myself frog-marched to a studio in another part of the building. I was seized by a sudden fit of trembling once I realised we were alone.

I was so very afraid, without a precise notion of what it was I had to fear, that I sank into a battered settee. I sat, petrified, my hands drawn around my knees, without life or spirit, not knowing how to look or how to stir. However, I fell into this state of stupefaction but briefly. The monster squatted by me and, without further ceremony or preamble, flung his arms about my neck, and drew me forcibly towards him, thus obliging me to receive, in spite of my struggles to disengage from him, his pestilential kisses, which quite overcame me.

Finding me next to senseless and unresisting, he tore down my Levi's, thus laying my secret places open to his hands and eyes. I endured this without flinching, till emboldened by my sufferance and silence, he attempted to lay me down on the settee, and I felt his hand on the lower part of my naked thighs. I hurriedly crossed my legs. While unbuttoning his filthy tweed breeks, he attempted to force my legs apart with his knee. I struggled and was losing ground when the brute gave up the fight, cursing the fact that he suffered from premature ejaculations.

Robin Goodfellow took my maidenhead. My friends importuned him to get me freed after I was charged with being drunk and disorderly. The constable responsible for my arrest despised culture. He imagined he was being mocked when I told him that what he took to be a pub crawl was actually art students creating a drinking sculpture. Serious work, dismemberment of things past. Now picture in your mind's eye a fair stripling between twenty-five and thirty, whose disordered curls irregularly shaded a face in the full roseate bloom of youth. Such was Robin Goodfellow, solicitor's clerk and aspirant rake.

Robin turned up at the police station and I was released into his custody. After my night in the cells, this blue-eyed Adonis saw his way to buying me a cooked breakfast. Eggs, chips, beans, mushrooms, fried slice and tomato, washed down with strong tea. Then he drove me to his bedsit in Toxteth. The walls were coated with grease from Robin's cooking. There were crumbs in the sheets. My saviour's impatience would not suffer him to undress me fully. He simply pulled down my knickers once I'd been manoeuvred onto my back. Half-dressed, he commenced the onset.

I complained that I could not bear the pain. Since I was an art student it hadn't occurred to Robin that I still possessed my virginity. I was forced to bear my distress with Robin's hand over my mouth. He pushed on until he shot his load. Even when Robin saw his sheets were splashed with blood he didn't twig that he'd spirited away my darling treasure, that hidden mine so eagerly sought by men, and which they never dig for but to destroy. After clocking the stained bedding, Robin sniggered that he wouldn't tongue me when I was menstruating.

Robin Goodfellow and I pleasured each other on numerous occasions, our cries shattering the stillness of night. The parting of the double ruby pout of his lips seemed to exhale an air sweeter and purer than that he drew in. What effort it cost me when I teasingly refrained from kissing him. A neck exquisitely graceful connected his head to a body of the most perfect form and vigorous constitution, in which all the strength of manhood was concealed and softened in appearance by the delicacy of his complexion, the smoothness of his skin, and the plumpness of his flesh.

The platform of his snow white breast presented on the vermilion summit of each pap the idea of a rose about to bloom. His shirt could not hinder me from observing the symmetry of his limbs, that exactness of shape, in the fall of it towards the loins, where the waist ends and the rounding swell of the hips commences; where the skin, sleek, smooth and dazzling white, burnished on the ripe flesh that crimped into dimples at the least pressure, that the touch could not rest upon, but slid over as on the surface of the most polished ivory.

Needing money to pay off debts, I resolved to transform prostitution into an art form. Martin Heidegger, a London gallery owner, felt unsure about the merits of my painting but was easily persuaded to give me an exhibition. He feigned an interest in ontology. Dasein. What I know is he scarce gave me breathing time between one encounter and the next. In the space of a few minutes he was in a condition for renewing the onset, to which, preluding with a storm of kisses, he drove the same course always, and with unabated fervour, kept me awake until dawn.

I substituted money for love as a way of attacking patriarchy. The kerb-crawlers who bought my favours were on an existential drive for authenticity. They styled themselves active nihilists and I took pleasure in undermining their desire to live passionately. Take Georges Sorel. When I saw him moved and fired for my purpose, I inflamed him more by asking several leading questions, such as: did he have a mistress? Was she prettier than me? Could he love a crack hoe like me? Of course, the blushing simpleton answered to my wish and set me up in a swank apartment.

Albert Camus was one of many marks who paid top whack to divest me of my virginity. Dressed as he was in panty hose beneath a business suit, this philosopher was one whom any woman might call a very pretty fellow. The madam of a brothel led me to Camus dressed in a white morning gown. My gown was loosened in a trice and I divested of it. My stay offered the next obstacle, which readily gave way. I was reduced to my shift, the plunging neckline of which gave his hands and eyes all the liberty they could wish.

In an instant my shift was drawn over my head and I stood naked before Camus. The philosopher placed me in a variety of postures, pointing out aspects of my beauty, with parentheses of kisses and what he announced as the inflammatory liberties of his hands which he said made all shame fly before them. Hurriedly exhausting the pleasures of regaling his sense of touch and sight, Albert found himself ungovernably wound up. He noisily availed himself of what he'd been tricked into believing was my virginity and the strains of love did not unduly delay my sleep that night.

Another oaf who availed himself of my much abused maidenhead was Gilles Deleuze. He was shown to my bedroom late at night with all the mysteries of silence and secrecy. I lay undressed and panting if not with the fears of a real maid, at least with those of a dissembled one – which gave me an air of confusion and bashfulness that was impossible to distinguish from the state being simulated, even by less partial eyes than those of this philosopher of desire. So let me abuse him as a cully, a mild reproach for such a psychologically-damaged man.

Adam objected that these "autobiographical" sketches merely documented my "fall" into prostitution, they provided no theoretical basis for claiming such activities were art. I cited the famous footnote from the *1844 Manuscripts. Prostitution is only a specific expression of the general prostitution of the labourer, and since it is a relationship into which falls not the prostitute alone, but also the one who prostitutes – and the latter's abomination is still greater – the capitalist, etc. also comes under this head.* Scald imperiously dismissed this quote by claiming Marx had never intended that it be published. I retaliated with *The Communist Manifesto.*

*Bourgeois clap-trap about the family and education, about the hallowed co-relation of parent and child, becomes more ridiculous, the more, by the action of Modern Industry, family ties among proletarians are torn asunder, and their children transformed into simple articles of commerce and instruments of labour. But you Communists would introduce community of women, screams the whole bourgeoisie in chorus. The bourgeois sees in his wife a mere instrument of production. Hearing that the instruments of* production are to be made common he can come to no other conclusion than that women likewise will be held in common.

He has not even a suspicion that the real point is to do away with the status of women as mere instruments of production. Nothing is more ridiculous than the virtuous indignation of our bourgeois at the community of women which, they pretend, is to be openly and officially established by the Communists. The Communists have no need to introduce community of women; it has existed almost from time immemorial. Our bourgeois, not content with having the wives and daughters of proletarians at their disposal, not to speak of common prostitutes, take the greatest pleasure in seducing each other's wives.

Bourgeois marriage is in reality a system of wives in common and thus, at the most, what the Communists might possibly be reproached with, is that they desire to introduce, in substitution for a hypocritically concealed, an openly legalised community of women. For the rest, it is self-evident that the abolition of the present system of production must bring with it the abolition of the community of women springing from that system, i.e., of prostitution both public and private. Scald dismissed this manifesto – co-authored with Engels – as a piece of leftist chicanery that was unworthy of serious study.

I rallied with a Charles Loudon citation about prostitutes from the *1844 Manuscripts*. The average life of these creatures after they have embarked on their career of vice is six or seven years. To maintain the number of sixty to seventy thousand prostitutes, there must be in the three kingdoms eight to nine thousand women who commit themselves to the profession each year, or about twenty-four each day – an average of one per hour; and if the same proportion holds good across the globe, there must constantly be in existence one and a half million women of this kind.

After Scald attacked communism as it had allegedly existed, I replied that not only was the Soviet Union a capitalist state and the organisational principles of bolshevism quintessentially anarchist – but also that democracy as it really existed left a lot to be desired. Adam then ventured into a defence of Tony Blair and New Labour. I counterattacked with a modified passage from 'The True Socialists'. New Labour has thrown off all blame from all individuals and shifted it to society, which is inviolable. *Cosi fan tutti*, it is finally only a matter of remaining good friends with all the world.

The characteristic aspect of prostitution, namely, that it is the most tangible exploitation – one directly attacking the physical body – of the proletariat by the bourgeoisie, the aspect where the "deed producing heartache" with its moral pauper's broth suffers bankruptcy, and where passion, class hatred thirsting for revenge, begins – this aspect is unknown to Tony Blair's New Labour. Instead these pricks bewail in prostitutes ruined grocers' assistants and small craftsmen's wives, in whom patriarchs can no longer admire "the masterpieces of creation", "beauty uncorrupted by sin", "the blossoms pervaded by the aroma of the holiest and sweetest feelings". *Pauvre petit bonhomme!*

Adam reiterated his belief that I'd no feeling for literature, that my attention was focused on second-rate texts from the nineteenth century. He sought to block what he mistook as the thrust of my argument by suggesting that next I'd be ping-ponging between Henry Mayhew and further selections of Engels, since I'd not yet culled anything from *The Condition Of The Working Class In England*. I insisted Mayhew wasn't archaic enough for me. Rather than setting ghosts walking, I sought to exalt new struggles and recover the spirit of revolution by invoking the example of long-dead generations.

Scald suggested Robert Burton's *The Anatomy Of Melancholy* might prove better medicine than appeals to Marx. When all other engines fail, that they can proceed no farther of themselves, their last refuge is to fly to bawds, panders, magical philters and receipts. By those means many a man is overcome and precipitated into this malady if he take not good heed. For these bawds are everywhere so common and so many, that, as they said of old Croton, all here either inveigle or be inveigled, we may say of our cities, there being so many professed, cunning bawds in them.

Besides bawdry is become an art, or a liberal science, as Lucian calls it; and there be such tricks and subtleties, so many nurses, old women, panders, letter-carriers, beggars, physicians, friars, confessors, employed about it, that no pen could recount it. Declaiming aloud three hundred verses would not suffice to tell the tale of your debaucheries. Such occult notes, steganography, polygraphy, nuntius animatus, or magnetical telling of their minds, which Cabeus the Jesuit, by the way, counts fabulous and false; cunning conveyances in this kind, that neither Juno's jealousy, nor Danae's custody, nor Argo's vigilancy can keep them safe.

Since I knew what was coming next, I cut Scald off

before he regaled me with a sectarian diatribe. Instead, I suggested John Stow's *Survey Of London* might prove a more worthy object of study. Unfortunately, while Stow deals with Bishopsgate and Shoreditch (Sewersditch), he doesn't write about prostitution in these districts. However, he docs broach this subject in connection to Bridge Ward Without, roughly matching the area we know as the Borough, which was then a part of Surrey. After listing five local jails and a number of notable houses, Stow gets down to the business that interests us.

On the west bank, next to the bear gardens where beasts were baited, was the Bordello, or Stewes, a row of brothels. In the eighth parliament of Henry II it was ordained and confirmed that divers whorehouses should be kept within that lordship or franchise, according to the old customs that had been established there time out of mind. These allowed stewe-houses had signs on their fronts, toward the Thames, not hanged out, but painted on the walls, as a Boar's Head, The Cross Keys, The Gun, The Castle, The Crane, The Cardinal's Hat, The Bell, The Swan, etc.

Reliable authorities say that prostitutes were forbidden the rites of the church so long as they continued in their liberated life-styles, and were excluded from

Christian burial if they were not reconciled to sexual repression before death. There was a plot of ground called the Single Women's Churchyard for the burial of these ewes, located away from the parish church. In 1546 the Southward stewes lost their privileges and were no longer to be used as brothels. At the King's command, the inhabitants of these buildings were to obey all the repressive laws then operative in his police state.

Changing the tack of our conversation, I asked Scald how he'd become interested in prostitution. The story he told was a literary echo, a fiction culled from the most obvious of sources. Adam claimed he'd been walking the streets of London seeking psychogeographical pleasures when he'd clocked an old maid selling flowers. He asked this street hawker where he might lodge that night. Being well pleased with his foolish urbanity, she promised to lead Scald to a warm bed. Ere long she'd lured the john into a bawdy house, which he recognised by the naked quines who surged around him.

Such tricks you will find in many places. In East London it was once common for a man to act as a pimp to his own wife. I poured a bourbon and mentioned Arthur Morrison's *A Child Of The Jago*, which is set in the slums that were demolished 100 years ago to make way for the estate where I now live. In his novel, Morrison describes women luring johns onto the Old Nichol where their men lay in wait to roll the bastards. Scald shook when I asked him if he'd ever been coshed or robbed by a prostitute.

Morrison's first book, a collection of short stories entitled *Tales Of Mean Streets*, created a sensation. By rights I should focus on the narrative that made Morrison a figurehead of literary realism. 'Lizrunt' relates the incidents that transform a factory girl into a prostitute plying her trade on Commercial Road. In the aftermath of the Jack The Ripper murders, one can understand why this tragic tale attracted interest. However, as far as *Tales Of Means Streets* goes, I prefer 'The Red Cow Group' – a satire which demolishes anarchism by describing Whitechapel deadbeats giving a self-styled incendiary a ghastly fright.

Adam sneered that he'd had enough of hacks. He wanted to talk about the man he considered the greatest master of the novel. He wanted to talk about Dickens. I'd read Dickens. I'd read Dickens until I was sick and it didn't take much from his pen to make me puke. Dickens gives his fullest depiction of what he maligns as the ruined woman in *David Copperfield*.

This book is difficult to read without immediately perceiving its faults and almost impossible to finish without feeling the utmost dislike for its author. *David Copperfield* is, after all, Dickens' most autobiographical work.

The story – but then story is hardly the right description for this sprawling bildungsroman in which a character like Mr. Micawber can be transformed from a sponger to a magistrate with the mere stroke of Dickens's pen – is an account of how the vissitudes of life have no effect whatsoever on its eponymous hero. This is a first person narrative, and Dickens (for Copperfield is Dickens) imagines that by presenting himself as optimistic and innocent, he will be found charming and likeable. The effect is merely grating, and the moral tone would be comic if Dickens were capable of humour.

In *David Copperfield*, Dickens gives prostitution the most considered treatment it receives in his fiction. But Dickens – with his mouth full of ash – is unable to state boldly what it is Little Emily might have become. Charles Copperfield (or David Dickens – give this mealy mouthed narrator what name you will) resorts to the rough reported speech of a fisherman to provide his readers with an intimation of the fate that awaits working girls seduced by their "betters". Dickens, of course, offers the family as a solution to such "corruption", which, closely read, means servants must know their station in life.

Little Emily come to London. She as had never seen it in her life. Alone. Without a penny. So Pretty. Almost the moment she lighted in the town, all so desolate, she found – so she believed – a friend. A decent woman spoke to her about the needlework she had been brought up to do, about finding plenty of it for her, about a lodging for the night, and making secret inquiration of me and all at home. When my child stood upon the brink of more than I can say or think on, true to her promise, Martha saved her.

Martha knew from bitter knowledge where to watch and what to do. She came, white and hurried, upon Emily in her sleep. She told her to rise up from worse than death. Them belonging to the house would have stopped her, but they might as soon have stopped the sea. Martha told them she was a ghost that called Emily from beside her open grave. She heeded no more what they said than if she had no ears. She walked among them with my child and brought her safe out, in the dead of night, from that pit of ruin!

This passage, this fantastic speech, all stage-fire and

no content, is the misjudged climax of Dickens' attempt to take on the world view of a defeated class in the name of a triumphant bourgeoisie. What Dickens didn't understand was that, in taking over elements of aristocratic culture, the bourgeoisie simultaneously transformed them. Money replaces honour and shame becomes relative. The tensions in Dickens' work, and there are few enough of them, stem from his desire to re-stage as easily-won victories battles in which the bourgeoisie had already triumphed, while perversely the cold logic of the cash nexus.

The house in which Little Emily eventually finds refuge was once fine but its costly old wood-work has been repaired with common deal. For Dickens, this is like the marriage of a reduced old noble to a plebeian pauper, with each party to the ill-assorted union shrinking away from the other. Such it was and such it would be for Dickens. He could only go backwards in his efforts to preserve a society that was rotten to its core. As a reformist, he was a reactionary: the models he worked with came from the past, the medieval era.

I poured more bourbon and reminded Adam that my chief interest was the relationship between quantity and quality, and how this manifested in the art of crime. Not all the tales I told were literary. Indeed, most were simply a slice of life, although a good many of these were gleaned secondhand. Working girls talk shop together, after all. One sort I'd befriended hailed from Aberdeen in Scotland. Before coming to London, Sarah had worked the maze of streets running from the top of Aberdeen harbour to the picturesque fishing village of Footdee, which constituted the city's red light district.

Close by the harbour are certain hotels much frequented by both oil workers and ladies of the night. After turning a trick in one of these establishments, Sarah was grabbed as she made her way down a corridor. The assailant had disguised himself by cutting eye and mouth holes in a duty free carrier, which he'd placed over his head. He wanted the thrill of not paying for sex with a whore. After dragging Sarah into a guest room, he attempted to rape her but she beat him off and ran down to the bar where someone called the cops.

Sarah knew that she'd been attacked on the fifth floor but had no idea which room the despoiler was occupying. The mystery was solved by a stroll around the hotel. The aspirant rapist had thrown the bag with which he'd disguised himself from the window of his room and, because it was a windless night, the grotesque mask rested directly beneath his lair. The fuzz were unusually methodical about their prosecution, since they were under pressure to halt an ongoing series of attacks on local prostitutes. Sarah's ravisher did time and she got compensation for the injuries she had suffered.

I then revealed my part in defrauding a wealthy city stockbroker who spent his Friday evenings in the company of East End whores. This man was jaded. Beating girls no longer pleased him. He wanted to do something more extreme. He was anxious to rape a bitch, any bitch, but couldn't countenance the disgrace if he was caught. I wasn't in direct contact with this fine gentleman but I came up with an ingenious solution to his conundrum. Lawful sex is a matter of consent. A woman willing to accommodate him but unable to consent might be raped without risk.

My colleagues cursed me for my college education. They said I spoke in riddles. I explained that a retarded adult with a mental age of five would be unable to consent to sex. Legally, a woman in this position couldn't assume responsibility for her actions. My compatriots complained that they didn't know any spastics. I told them not to worry, any woman who was unknown to the gentleman in question might pretend to be backward. Since this rake was, or had been, familiar with everyone present except me, my associates took great delight in electing *moi* to play this role

The lecher was greatly pleased by the proposed scheme of rape. So pleased that he wanted to make his debauching of a retard something unnaturally special. In short, I was to be driven to his pile in Essex where he might have me on his creaking marital bed while his unsuspecting wife attended an evening prayer meeting in Chelmsford. We (that is to say, me and the two harlots who posed as my procurers) decided to make a day of the trip. The blackguard lived in Danbury, so in the early morning we drove to the nearby town of Maldon.

Historic Maldon. Now, that caught my listener's interest, since he knew the place name was a corruption of the Anglo-Saxon word *Maeldum*, meaning a cross on a hill top. Adam had never visited the town, but knew it was the site of the famous Battle of Maldon where Earl Bryhtnoth met military defeat at the hands of the Danes in 991. This event is recorded in the earliest extant Saxon epic poem. What Adam did not know was that delightful Maldon gained its Royal Charter in 1171 and during the eighteenth century was the second biggest town in Essex.

Adam wanted me to describe the place as I'd seen it, so I did this by listing the shops I saw on my visit. The Cycle Store. Francine's Restaurant. Ideal Phones. Damon (women's clothes). Ansells Butchers. Manor Frames. Foremost Insurance. Friars Pottery. Saffron Tea Rooms. Abbotts Estate Agents. Wheelers Fish & Chips. Taylors Estate Agents. Alliance & Leicester Building Society. Landmark Estate Agents. Point Graphics. World Choice Travel. Blue Boar Hotel. The Old Cutting Rooms (hairdresser). Noel Health and Beauty. Cantelec Electrical Goods. Jonathan Vine (menswear). Platform One (women's clothes). Ben's House (record shop). Talking Flowers. The Kit Room (sports). Jabberwocky Gifts.

Adam told me that my description of Maldon was prosaic. I rejoined that it might have been scientific if he'd given me time to fill in a few more businesses, such as Mitchell, Caulkett & Coiley the solicitors. Located at a distance of fifty miles from London, Maldon had avoided the thousand cuts of commuter towns. Day trippers were attracted to the Blackwater Estuary, hence the plethora of restaurants and fast food joints. The charity shops sold an uninspiring selection of secondhand goods but All Books was a well stocked used book store. I'd had a good day in the town.

My confederates and I moved on after an excess of eating, shopping and riverside recreations. Adam didn't want to know that the iron age hill fort known as Danbury Camp rises 111 metres above sea level. I simply told him that we parked a discreet distance from the rake's house. When we got to his front door, I screamed I wanted an ice cream and stuck my thumb in my mouth. It wasn't a difficult act to keep up and the pervert blithely paid five thousand pounds cash for sex with what he believed to be a severely retarded woman.

I poured more bourbon and refrained from mentioning that I'd noted how aroused Adam had become during the course of my tale. I suspected this was what caused him to interrupt my attempt at an exhaustive list of the businesses operative in Maldon. This topographical description had definitely excited him. It is well known that almost anything can become erotically charged through processes of association. Likewise, the way in which commodities acted as advertisements for capitalism resulted in a close association between sex and shopping. Indeed, we are conditioned by the very mechanisms of the market to make this link.

When I've been drinking, my thoughts often wander off a subject and then return to it. I wasn't surprised therefore to find myself contemplating the relentless and repetitive recourse to images of prostitution in anti-capitalist discourse. In connection with this, I mentioned a newspaper review of a text written by a police spy called Hodde, in which Marx observed: the masses of paint and patchouli under which prostitutes try to smother the less attractive aspects of their existence have their literary counterpart in the bel esprit with which de la Hodde perfumes his pamphlet. Adam stopped up his ears.

Adam kept his fingers in his ears as I vocalised – from memory, I might add: my memory runs along peculiar lines when I'm drunk – the famous passage in *The Eighteenth Brumaire* where Marx describes the lumpenproletariat. Decayed roués with doubtful means of subsistence and of doubtful origin, ruined offshoots of the bourgeoisie eager for adventures, vagabonds. discharged soldiers, discharged jail-bird, escaped galley-slaves, swindlers, mountebanks, lazzaroni, pickpockets, tricksters, gamblers, procurers, brothel-keepers, porters, literaten, organ-grinders, rag-pickers, knife grinders, tinkers, beggars, in short the whole indefinite, disintegrated mass thrown hither and thither, which the French term la bohème.

The notion of escaped galley-slaves forming a constituent part of la bohème tickles me as rhetoric, and while this is a clear indication that the passage under discussion should not be taken literally, nevertheless the inclusion of tinkers illustrates Marx was capable of base and irrational prejudice. That said, I believe cabbies would have been inserted alongside porters if Marx was writing today, since many hackney carriage operators are former police officers with racist attitudes. I mentioned this conviction to Adam, who having removed his fingers from his ears to take up his bourbon was perplexed by the remark.

I added that, with his usual bombast, Dickens once wrote: What an interesting book a hackney-coach might produce. The autobiography of a broken down hackney coach would surely be as amusing as the autobiography of a broken down hackneyed dramatist; and it might tell as much of its travels. How many stories might be related of the different people it had conveyed on matters of business or profit, pleasure or pain. And how many melancholy tales of the same people at different periods. The country-girl, the showy over-dressed woman, the drunken prostitute, the dissipated spendthrift, the thief.

Rather than letting Adam know that I was free-associating around a list encompassing procurers and brothel-keepers, I refocused on another text about 1848: 'The Class Struggles In France'. (I know of course that Alexander Herzen also wrote on these events, but I find it impossible to treat his feuilleton *From The Other Shore* any more seriously than hack work by Dickens.) Returning to Marx and 'The Class Struggles In France' – and trying hard not to slur my words – I explained that, in this text, a society of disorder, prostitution and theft is said to stand behind Louis Napoleon.

I had not forgotten that, in this article, Marx calls up images of prostitutes in his condemnation of aestheticism. Not the real Paris but the idle Paris now thronging with its lackeys, its blacklegs, its literary bohème, its cocottes. The civil war but an agreeable diversion, eyeing the battle through telescopes, and swearing by their own honour and that of their whores that the performance was far better got up than it used to be. The men who fell were really dead; the cries of the wounded were cries in earnest; and, besides, the whole thing was so intensely historical.

Marx's prose was often heavy handed and clumsy, but it contained poetry too. Marx represented the best and the worst of his age. But Adam wasn't interested. He wanted me to excite him with tales of my work as a prostitute. So I gave him a story mediated by a literary tradition he didn't recognise, because it pre-dated Samuel Richardson. It ran from Thomas Nashe and Robert Greene through Francis Kirkman's *The Counterfeit Lady Unveiled* to Defoe. It even encompassed prurient works of piety such as John Dunton's *The Night Walker: or, Evening Rambles in Search after Lewd Women.*

There was a free jazz and blues concert in Hyde Park which I attended with the intention of insinuating myself into wealthy company. I entered a beer tent; this was a thing of no great consequence to me and not much came of it until a well-dressed businessman began to feel the effects of what he'd consumed and in his frequent talk with all those present, he gradually singled me out and was very particular with me. He told me he would pay for my drinks, and did so; which gave him leave to continue his parlay with me.

He held me in talk so long, till at last he drew me out of the beer tent and we walked through the park to Oxford Street. Arm in arm we talked of a thousand things cursorily without any apparent purpose. Eventually the businessman said he was charmed with my company and asked me if I dared trust myself in a chauffeur-driven car with him. The suit insisted he was a man of honour and would not try anything unbecoming. I seemed to decline it a while but suffered myself to be importuned a little more and then yielded.

At first I didn't know what this gentleman designed, but I soon discovered that having had too much to drink, he was keen to down more. His chauffeur drove us to a restaurant in Knightsbridge, where he treated me to a meal while he drank freely. He pressed me to drink but I declined saying I felt randy and that if he was man enough to satisfy my lust then I wanted to preserve the memory of it. Once I'd eaten my fill, he called for our bill, settled with a credit card and hurried me out to his car.

The businessman fondled me in the car but didn't push things on the back seat, where we could be seen by his chauffeur. The driver was instructed to stop at a house where we were shown to an upstairs room with a bed in it. Here the businessman began to be a little freer with me until little by little I yielded to everything, so that, in a word, he did what he pleased with me. I need say no more. All this while he drank freely too, and about eleven in the evening we went down to his car.

A full day of drinking and the motion of the car made the businessman ready to act out again what he'd just done before, but this time in view of his chauffeur.

Thinking my game secure, I resisted him. Instead I made him lay his head on my lap and within five minutes he was fast asleep. Since the rear view mirror was intended for viewing cars behind us, the chauffeur couldn't see what went on beneath the level of my breasts without turning around. Thus I felt confident I would not be observed as I searched my prostrate companion.

I took a gold watch, a fat wallet, his tooled leather shoes, gold cuff links, mobile phone, silver cigarette case, a reef of papers and some keys. The driver pulled up at some red lights in the Strand and I jumped out, and after closing the door was immediately swallowed by the crowd swarming around Charing Cross train station. The chauffeur shouted after me but not knowing his master had been robbed and thinking I was just a drunken tart, let me go without crying thief. I walked down to the river and then along the Embankment to Temple tube.

I stepped onto an eastbound train reflecting that there is nothing more ridiculous than a drunk man who gives himself up to lust. He is possessed by two devils at once and can no more act according to reason than a Ford Escort can run without fuel. His vice tramples upon his cunning and he is blinded by his own rage. He will pick up a woman without regard to who she is or what she is, regardless of whether she is ugly or pretty, old or young, and he is too blind to distinguish another drunk from a thief.

Such a man is worse than a lunatic. He no more knows what he is doing than the wretch I'd just robbed knew that I'd lifted his watch and his wallet. I rejoiced in the fact that such gentlemen did not consider the contempt they were held in. The cunning jade thinks of no pleasure but money, and when her victim is drunk with sexual passion, her hands are in his pockets searching for what she can find there, and of which he can no more be sensible in the moment of his folly than he can forfeit loose women.

Adam pressed his hands uneasily against his pockets, so I told him I knew a woman who was so dextrous with her fingers that while a john had his way with her, she conveyed a leather wallet with two hundred pounds in it out of his fob-pocket and replaced it with a plastic substitute filled with waste paper. After he'd come, the john accused her of picking his pocket. She jested that he didn't have much to lose. The john put his hand to his fob and feeling a stuffed wallet released the central locking system on his motor.

Having unsettled Adam, I returned to the thrust of

my narrative. I got off the tube at Aldgate East and wandered into Wentworth Street so that I might turn some tricks. A car pulled up but there is no way I'd get into a motor with four youths. It isn't unusual for prostitutes to be assaulted and robbed. Not long before, a seventeen year-old runaway had been picked up by two men in Kings Cross, raped, pillaged and thrown naked from a car on Quaker Street. I made it a strict rule only to do business with solitary johns,

Staying well away from the car, I offered to sell the teenagers the mobile I'd stolen. I told them I'd just lifted it from a lush and they'd get a good many calls from it before its unconscious owner realised it was missing. The boys were interested, one of them opened a side door, but as I held the phone up it rang. The car pulled away from the kerb, the opened door wasn't slammed shut until it reached the junction with Osbourne Street. The scene was truly surreal, since the mobile's ringing tone was an electronically castrated Beethoven melody.

I answered the call and wasn't entirely surprised to discover the gentleman I'd robbed on the other end of the line. The fact that I'd mugged him only inflamed this soak to further sexual passions. He wanted to meet me straight away but I said he should cool his heels overnight. He said I could keep the money I'd stolen from him – several hundred pounds – and he'd pay me for sex and the return of the other things I'd taken. I was wary in case he was laying a trap and told him to call me sometime the next afternoon.

At this juncture I decided it was best to place the phone in safe hands. I spoke to another working girl and asked if anyone had been arrested for soliciting earlier that night. Someone I knew to be quite trustworthy – she turned tricks in order to earn extra money for her kids and didn't have a habit – had been lifted. I went to her flat. A baby-sitter let me in and I paid her off. My friend wasn't long getting home. I got her to take the mobile and made her promise to deal with whatever calls came in.

The next day my friend took a call from the fine gentleman who'd treated me to dinner the previous night. On the phone she denied all knowledge of my robbery. I'd instructed her to say the mobile had been put through her letter box with a note attached saying she should wait for a call from a man who wanted a whore, which was what she'd done. My friend named her price – the figure was ten times her usual fee – and said if the caller wanted to visit her flat, she would give him instruction on how to get there.

The lecher laid out his money and fucked my friend. However, what he wanted was not simply to buy back his property, but the chance to shag me stupid. He was told this information might be put out on the criminal grapevine and his property would be procured quite easily. However, inducing the woman who'd rolled him to risk a second encounter was a course of action fraught with difficulties. The businessman bought his phone back from my confidant and paid her hand- somely for it, not only to demonstrate his good will but so she could call him on it.

The next day my associate took the lecher's gold watch to his office in the city. He gave her five hundred pounds for it, which was more than I would have got from a pawnbroker, although it was worth much more. The businessman asked after his credit cards, papers and keys. A few days later my friend carried these items into the city and received three thousand pounds for her trouble – which we split evenly between us. The businessman tried to discover if my partner knew who I was, but she insisted she'd obtained the loot from a male fence.

I often thought about seeing the businessman but wasn't sorry I'd refused to do so on the phone. Since my go-between remained unmolested by the police, after a month I decided it was safe to call my masochistic admirer. He was desperate to see me and although my price was extremely steep, I think he would have paid more. He drove alone to Wentworth Street and picked me up in a car. The first time we did this I had sex with him and then made off on foot, later on I let him come back to my flat.

We had these encounters once a week for a year. However, he never came into a settled way of maintenance with me, which is what would have best pleased me. Eventually he got caught up in some Christian cult and then his visits became less frequent. Sometimes he would rave about my wicked life-style, and then I wouldn't see him for a month. Then his lust would get the better of him and he'd come back to me. That was, until he became engaged to a woman who attended his church, and after that I never saw him again.

Scald enjoyed this tale, but we'd reached an impasse. The only place Adam could go now was backwards. There was nowhere else to go. I'd no desire to take up Richardson, since what could I do with the likes of Mrs. Sinclair beyond noting her stunted relationship to my interests? From Richardson, we might have worked through to Joyce if Scald had been willing to admit he'd found my portrait of Maldon smutty because it reminded him of the detailed description of Bloom's drawers in *Ulysses*. Why, I'd not even reached the Maldon Crystal Salt Company in my abortive mapping!

It would be wrong to view Adam's failure to grasp the historical dimensions of his chosen art as ironic. What Richardson did was hold a mirror to the middle classes and reflect back an image they almost recognised as their own. The audience for *Pamela* and *Clarissa* was like an infant who, upon gazing into a glass, doesn't quite recognise his or her reflection. This was narcissism, for real self-love requires types of self-understanding the bourgeois subject does not possess. If the novel required a subtle handling of time, it is now time to move beyond the novel.

This was exactly what Adam – a typical member of the chattering classes – could not do. He wanted to hang onto a moment that was lost and reproduce it through works of fiction. His interest in the domestic led him to seek out its other in the form of prostitution – not as a paradigmatic example of class exploitation – but to confirm the essentialised femininity of the sensitive male artist he'd constructed as his identity. Scald was attempting to mark time without confronting the effects of the Puritan rotation. He was loathe to admit that historical reasoning necessarily entails confrontations with power.

Scald was so passive in his consumption of cultural stereotypes that he was unable to see that his literary models – Fielding and Dickens, with their preference for plotting over characterisation – were a perfect cul-de-sac even from the point of view of bourgeois aesthetics. Jane Austin provided better fare for those immersed in a seriousness that led to the scrutiny of the steam given off by kettles and the intricacies of marriage contracts. Kettle steam did provide a fine example of the relationship between quantity and quality but, like Frank Leavis, Adam was blind to the effects of condensation.

While I'd been contemplating the way in which quantitatively increasing the temperature of water will eventually produce a qualitative transformation, Scald had got steamy. He pressed a score into my hand and, once I'd salted the money away, instructed me to fondle the aspect of his personage that was swelling with desire. My fingers touched it and closed upon it. It lolled in my immodest grip. Adam exposed his belly and moaned plaintively. His appurtenance throbbed and lengthened miraculously in my hand. Thinking I'd find French saucy, he called me *mademoiselle*, then *ma petite belle*. His accent was shockingly poor.

I gaped at the extremity while maintaining the friction demanded for my reckoning. There was a wrinkled sack below, which wagged about as I frigged. I grasped the loose skin that could no longer cover his plum. I pressed it back at each movement. *Je vais jouir!* My strokes grew quicker. I moved my right hand up and down as if I was milking a cow. Suddenly a stream of hot spunk sprayed over my hand and along my arm, reaching up as far as my neck. I kept jerking until the froth-coated appendage slipped from my sticky fingers.

I poured more bourbon and Scald mumbled something about *Esther Waters* by George Moore. The book was once notorious for passages describing childbirth, but from my point of view the very slight interest I took in this work derived from chapter twenty one, where Moore's eponymous heroine rejects the idea of becoming a prostitute. Despite Moore's having been scandalously influenced by French Realism in his earlier novels, *Esther Waters* was coy even in comparison to Zola's Nana. James Joyce judiciously condemned *Esther Waters* as the best modern novel of English life. A classic example of damning something with faint praise.

Adam wanted to maintain the illusion that prostitutes choose their trade from inclination rather than economic necessity. His belief that one kind of wage-slavery was preferable to another, or indeed was a subject of choice, was absurd. Likewise, the very literature he'd consumed warning that recourse to bawds would endanger his health had served to inflamed the passions of this ethically-inclined hypocrite. A woman like me whose quiver was open to every arrow, who liked all who had fat purses and loved none who were destitute, was a dangerous troll to be fucked and condemned as a pollutant.

I was neither for nor against prostitution. My artistic model in projecting these archaic images of the whore insolently back at the society which produced them was Borani, the legendary anti-painter of the eighteenth-century who was paid to whitewash the medieval murals decorating Saint-Denis, Tours, Angers and Chartres cathedrals. Malevitch could spin in his grave; whiting out the artistic triumphs of a previous age put to shame both white-on-white and black-on-black. I cared not one whit for conventional histories of the avant-garde. Putting an end to tradition necessitated intransigence towards the past.

Adam was spent, and so, to revive him, I announced that the crossbiting law was a public profession of shameless cozenage mixed with incestuous whoredoms. The method of this mischievous art was for a harlot to yield her body up to a man, it being arranged that a third party should appear and, finding them in bed together, demand money to prevent an unpleasant scene with the adulterous woman's husband. The crossbiting law has been called the badger game by more recent practitioners such as Chicago May, Dutch Gus and Kid McManus, but I much preferred the sixteenth-century term.

There are many men who, having inflamed their lust with lager, find their eyes falling upon the painted faces of Commercial Street. Chicago May used the term "mark", but in Elizabethan London victims of the crossbiting law were called "simplers". Beyond violence, a single man has little to fear from the pretended husband of a crossbiting bitch, and the ready cash he might part with is usually no more than several hundred pounds. Politicians, celebrities and priests make the best simplers – particularly if they are married or prone to droning on about morality. From such men I've extorted fantastic sums.

By this time, the bottle of bourbon was empty and I was well and truly caned. I demanded that Adam tell me about his research into prostitution but, even after overcoming a certain reticence on his part, the results were not at all promising. Scald told me of an English vicar's daughter he'd encountered in a Tokyo brothel during the course of his investigation into sex tourism. Sophie had grown up in rural Lincolnshire and at the age of eighteen found herself pursued by two suitors. The first disqualified himself by warning the girl against the artifices of his rival.

Having dropped John Smith for his priggery and bitching, Sophie promptly allowed herself to be seduced by the wide-girthed David Jones, whose legendary ugliness led her to pity him. David's attempted abduction of the girl failed but it might well have succeeded if Smith had not enjoyed a certain influence over the two ladies – as Jones called them – who were, in fact, abandoned women from Skegness, without breeding or pity, who'd been employed to decoy Sophie to London. Jones owed his eventual triumph to Sophie's hope of driving this unhappily deranged man back along the path of Christian Righteousness.

Sophie knew that the ceremony of her marriage, which was privately performed by a defrocked paedophile, was in no way binding, and that she had nothing to trust to but David's honour. However, she soon discovered Jones had been married already, by the same priest, to eight other teenagers – six of them beneath the age of consent – who, like Sophie, he had deceived and then turned to prostitution. The day after her marriage, Sophie had been taken to a brothel where she'd met two unhappy girls, who like her had been deceived and pimped to other men for David's profit.

Sophie was desperate to win Jones for Jesus and so, unable to bear rivals for his affections, strove to forget her infamy in a tumult of pleasures. With this in view, she danced and talked lewdly, but still was unhappy. The gentlemen who visited the seraglio often praised the power of Sophie's charms but this only contributed her melancholy. Thus, with each day, she grew more pensive and more insolent, until at last the monster Jones had the temerity to offer her to a young business-man. Her resistance was madness and she found herself shipped to Japan as a concubine.

Adam's tale depressed me, so I told him I'd recently travelled to Gravesend. Making my way on foot I passed a man who'd picked me up in Spitalfields the night before. He was loading golf clubs into a Nissan and told me he was participating in a local tournament, but if I came back after dark and went into his garage where we could have sex in his car, he'd pay me well. I agreed to this and once the john drove off, knocked on the door of his house, thinking I might rob it if no-one was in.

A middle-aged woman answered my summons, so I asked her about the state of her marriage and she was happy to pay me to provide her with grounds for getting divorced. I took five hundred pounds from the wife and went away. The abused spouse contacted a private detective who, armed with an infra-red camera, concealed himself in the garage. The golf enthusiast was lurking in the front garden when I returned to his family home after dark. We did the business in his Nissan and I earned a pony for these exertions. I wasn't required in court.

Adam wasn't impressed by my story, so, to inflame him, I asked a rhetorical question. How much profit grows from whores? Rather than waiting for Scald to reply, I announced with a flourish that kerb-crawlers needed cars and that these chariots required both petrol and servicing, therefore the motor industry would be much diminished without the extra trade streetwalkers generated. Similarly, the medical profession required patients. Without sexually transmitted diseases – and hookers are a great repository of the pox – the occupation would be crippled. Likewise, the beauty industry would crash without innumerable ragged whores splattering their faces with cosmetics.

Not being literate enough to recognise that, like Marx, I'd plundered Robert Greene's *A Disputation* for a very hoary joke about political economy, Adam was impressed. He became excited, perhaps too excited and began ranting incoherently about his admiration for Henry James. He invoked the image of New York City as a seraglio that welled fantastically out of a piece of travel writing. There was the charged atmosphere in James, the barely repressed sexual energy and metaphors that crackled through everything he'd written. James was a man obsessed with abandoned shoes and what might be glimpsed furtively through a keyhole.

I'd been trying to avoid the Victorian period – but thanks to all its historic resonances, this was what the matter of London always drew the psychohistorian towards, or rather, forced her to fight against. Like so many other writers, Scald was unable to go either backwards or forwards. I knew I couldn't draw him ahead but it was just as difficult to pull him rearwards. I mentioned that, alongside Nashe and Greene, it was Thomas Dekker who'd produced the most illuminating pamphlets about Elizabethan low-life – specifically citing *Lanthorne & Candle-Light: Being Part II of The Belman of London* (1608).

Adam objected that he'd only heard of Dekker as a playwright. Having constituted himself as a bourgeois subject, Scald insisted on projecting his own limitations as a universally valid "human condition". In vain did I recount by heart divers passages from chapter nine of Dekker's *Lanthorne* – 'The Infection Of The Suburbs'. Beelzebub keeps the register book of all the bawds, panders and courtesans – and he knows that these suburb sinners have no lands to live upon but their legs. Every apprentice passing by them can say, there sits a whore. How happy therefore were cities if they had no suburbs.

Dekker might have taken us forwards, it was certainly curious that a writer as inept as JG Ballard should be one of the few novelists to view the relationship between city and suburb as objectively as Dekker – even if his moral position was an inversion of TD's overdone pieties. Since Adam insisted sixteenth and seventeenth century prose was unworthy of his attention, I turned the conversation to plays apparently written in verse – *Volpone, A Chaste Maid In Cheapside, 'Tis A Pity She's A Whore.* But Scald objected that Shakespeare was the only writer of that period who interested him.

Doll Tearsheet was quickly exhausted as a subject of conversation; Adam insisted that he'd rather talk of her familiar Falstaff. So James was his topic of choice and James it would be. I soon learnt to my terror that Scald was obsessed by both James and his theme. He could talk of little else, and it wasn't the prose fiction that interested him. Rather, the sexual obsessions in the work were the point from which Adam first came to hit on the man as a truly historical figure – rewritten in Scald's mind from bon vivant to world famous serial killer.

Adam wanted to unfold his subject in the manner of the master – but his approach lacked subtlety and sureness of touch. He used a rhetorical question. Just what was James doing on 31 August 1888? Then another. What was James doing on 8 September 1888? And this the last. What was James doing on 30 September 1888? I replied there had been five murders, the double homicide being represented by 30 September, so the events of 9 November must be raised. Scald called me a fool. The first four murders took place outside, the last indoors; there were two killers.

As Adam ranted, I searched through some cupboards and unearthed a bottle of Vina Mara Rioja (Californian wine), which I opened. Scald was rabbiting about a letter Henry James had written to his brother William from Geneva on 29 October 1888. In this missive, James wrote of suddenly becoming conscious around 10 October of his need to get away from London – and more specifically, Whitechapel. The Jack the Ripper slayings were commonly known as the Whitechapel murders and Scald asked why a writer who lived in Chelsea would travel abroad to avoid a district located ten miles from his home.

Adam was satisfied that he already knew the answer to his questions. James was Jack the Ripper. As one might expect from a man so incontestably bourgeois as Scald, his research was anything but thorough. It soon became apparent that he was overly reliant on the three volumes of *Henry James Letters* edited by Leon Edel. He had done little to locate epistles excluded from the Edel selection. He had, however, supplemented his knowledge of the Letters with Edel's *Henry James: A Life* and several lesser biographies such as those by Harry T Moore, H Montgomery Hyde and Lyndell Gordon.

Precisely because Adam used the James letters as evidence – and his case rested on an over-literal interpretation of the reference to Whitechapel – he wished to finger this writer as the Ripper on the basis of four of the five homicides traditionally attributed to the fiend. If we accept what James writes as true, he couldn't have murdered Mary Kelly in her Dorset Street lodgings on 9 November 1888 because he wasn't in England. Scald emphasised that eleven East End prostitutes were murdered between 3 April 1888 and 13 February 1891 and the Ripper was not behind all the slayings.

I tried to tell Scald his solution to the murders was unsatisfactory but he interrupted me, dismissing my objections before I could lay them before him. Stephen Knight in *Jack The Ripper: The Final Solution* fingered the painter Walter Sickert for all five of the Whitechapel murders. Knight's tale made a good story, but he failed to prove his case. Still, Scald lacked even a motive beyond sexual frenzy and, while fitting up a famous writer as the Ripper had the makings of a bestseller, the reading public would demand a solution that nailed him for all five murders.

If I'd been Scald, I'd have claimed that James – knowing that the police suspected him of the Ripper crimes – laid a false trail in his letters and other reports of his movements. Thus he tricked his sister Alice into thinking he'd gone to Switzerland for an assignation with the bluestocking Constance Fenimore Woolson.

Indeed, I'd allow that James probably did meet up with Woolson – but returned secretly to London by 9 November 1888, and was indeed responsible for butchering Mary Jane Kelly. That way, James would be responsible for all five murders, and the requirements of a bestselling book satisfied.

The letter to Francis Boott of 18 January 1889, in which James outlines his recent travels, is best attacked head-on as vague and contradictory. In writing that he visited Monte Carlo (just two months previously), it is peculiar that he should claim he spent two or three weeks at the resort – a discrepancy of sufficient magnitude to arouse suspicion. Likewise, James insists he returned from abroad on Christmas Eve – but three sentences later contradicts himself by writing he spent the month of December in Paris, and this after testifying he was in England during the final week of December.

Stephen Knight's solution to the Whitechapel murders was attractive precisely because it implicated a famous artist while providing a motive – covering up a royal scandal – rather than simply assuming the killer was a deranged maniac. Knight's explanation seduced his readers rather than convincing them, a necessary strategy in a case where the sheer volume of specula-

tion and false trails meant that the identity of the mur-
derer could never be resolved to the satisfaction of all
those who'd made an emotional investment in it. The
Jack the Ripper murders were a mini-industry fed by
sensationalism rather than sober historical evaluation.

It would be easy to adapt elements of Knight's thesis
and apply them to James. The idea that James was
privy to a secret aristocratic scandal is plausible.
Likewise, it is possible James fucked whores and inadvertently revealed something to a prostitute that she
then spread amongst other sex workers. To prevent
loose talk becoming a full blown scandal, James might
have found it necessary to become a serial killer. This
might begin to explain not only the Whitechapel
murders but also something of the mature Jamesian
style – both were necessitated by his need to excise the
indelicacies of 1888.

For several minutes I was so absorbed in my own
thoughts that I didn't take in what Adam was saying,
then suddenly his words hit me with the force of a
flood. Scald ranted that De Quincey's Society of
Connoisseurs in Murder was a fictional representation
of a genuine literary club that had been founded during
the reign of George III and still existed today. Members
not only discussed homicides, they committed them.

James Boswell had established the fraternity to slaughter prostitutes after he'd caught clap from a courtesan called Louisa as described in his *London Journal* of 1762-1763.

Adam directed my attention to encounters with prostitutes which Boswell recorded in *Journal* entries dated 26 November and 4 December 1762; and then those for 12 January, 25 & 31 March, 13 April, 10, 17, 19 & 31 May, 4, 10 & 18 June, and 4 August 1763. Personally, I wasn't convinced by the evidence Scald claimed proved Samuel Johnson's biographer got his rocks off by murdering prostitutes. Adam insisted that the references to the murder and mutilation of whores were coy – as were intimations of a friendship with the radical politician John Wilkes – because Boswell knew British intelligence might seize his diary.

Scald seemed to be drawing on inside information when he cackled that the wrong man was jailed for the Yorkshire Ripper slayings, since the real killer was a famous literary figure. I began to worry that Adam was fronting a literary club dedicated to audacious sex crimes. The fact that Scald insisted only sex murders committed in the street constituted a genuine art form was not particularly reassuring. My head was lolling on my chest, I'd fallen into a drunken slumber in my chair but something made me start up. A low, piteous howling of dogs somewhere near my flat.

Louder rang the howls as I looked up at the uncurtained window, and the floating motes of dust I could see took new shapes to the sound as they danced in the moonlight. I felt myself struggling to awake to some call of my instincts. Nay, my very soul was struggling, and my half-remembered sensibilities were striving to answer the call. I was succumbing to self-hypnosis! Quicker and quicker danced the dust. The moonbeams quivered as they went by me into the mass of gloom beyond. More and more they gathered till they took on dim phantom shapes.

And then I started, broad awake and in full possession of my self-hypnotised senses. I stifled a scream in my throat. I was not alone and I must take control. The room was the same, unchanged in any way since I came into it. I could see along the floor, in the brilliant moonlight, my own footsteps marked where I had disturbed the long accumulation of dust. Scald's deep, burning eyes seemed set amongst swollen flesh, for the lids and pouches underneath were bloated. It seemed as if the whole awful creature were simply gorged with innocent women's blood.

He lay exhausted with his repletion. Pissed as a fart.

I shuddered as I bent over to touch him and every sense in me revolted at the contact, but I had to search or I was lost. The coming night might see my own body a banquet in a similar way to those poor victims of James Boswell and Jack the Ripper. I felt all over Adam's bulk, but no sign could I find of his wallet. Then I stopped and looked at the Scald. There was a mocking smile on the bloated face which seemed to drive me mad.

Adam struck me as a maniac who considered London a backdrop against which he could satiate his lusts while recruiting an ever-widening circle of literary butchers to batten on helpless prostitutes. The very thought drove me mad. I pushed the drunk forwards in his chair and found his wallet in a back pocket. As I pulled it free, Scald's eyes rolled open. The last glimpse I had was of the bloated face with a grin of malice which would have held its own in the nethermost hell. My brain seemed on fire and I ran screaming from my flat.

I got down one flight of stairs before being grabbed – not by Scald who had failed to follow me – but by Amy Smith, a crack hoe who lived in the flat beneath mine. She had a john who wanted three way fucking, so she dragged me into her pad to help fulfil his fantasies. Amy threw me into her chamber where the trick – who turned out to be the pop singer Jim Morrison – was tucked into the bed. Amy sat me down, pulled off my shoes and stockings, and my other clothes, piece by piece, before leading me to Morrison.

After the fright I'd received from Scald, I found myself unable to resist Amy as she shamelessly thrust me into her double bed. While my aesthetic practice necessitated that I turn tricks, at that moment I was in no state to service a john. I would have got up from the mattress had Morrison not pulled me against him and threatened to get his road crew to gang rape me if I resisted his will. Since he held me fast, I lay still and let him do what he would. Jim was nonplussed by my sudden submission and went flaccid.

Amy got into bed with us and tried to excite Morrison. This brought on performance anxiety and he failed to get it up. Soon afterwards, he attempted to leave without paying and Amy had to use a switchblade to gain possession of his purse. When I mentioned there was a john in my flat, she hissed I should have said so earlier. Amy announced she'd turn the trick and bounded away before I could stop her. Que sera sera. I dressed and ran down to the street where, revived by the night air, I went in search of a party.

Coming out of Old Nichol Street, I crossed Shoreditch High Street and wandered down New Inn Yard, then up Great Eastern Street. At the junction where Charlotte Road lay to my right and Leonard Street to my left, there were cabbies illegally parked up and touting for business like flies swarming around a fresh turd. No, I didn't want a taxi, I lived around the corner. This was the new Shoreditch, with yuppies pouring out of the Great Eastern Dining Rooms and the Cantaloupe. The art and club crowd favoured the Bricklayers Arms just a smidgen further along Charlotte Road.

Trendies went for The Dragon Bar and Home Bar, both on Leonard Street. I'd always thought Home was a stupid name for a drinking establishment; after all, I went out to get away from home. The street was heaving but with a very different crowd from those who'd have patronised Edward Alleyn's Fortune Theatre which had stood nearby in Elizabethan times. I only had to make my way towards the Barbican and not only would I get away from the crowds but I'd be approaching the original Grub Street. Way back when Hoxton was rendered Hogstown, the area was disreputable.

I shouldered my way up Charlotte Road, still

crowded despite the horde of taxi drivers desperate to fleece anyone stupid enough to be taken for a ride. The 333 didn't appeal, the club was supposedly trendy but I'd preferred the London Apprentice – a gay bar – which it had replaced. The 333 attracted teenagers and to my eyes the popular night spot looked like a youth club. Behind it, on Hoxton Square, the Lux Cinema had closed for the night and I felt little inclination to try the Hoxton Bar or the London Electricity Show Rooms. I'd go to Charlie Wrights.

I made my way to Pitfield Street. Being a single woman I didn't have any trouble gaining entry to Charlie Wrights International Bar. I charmed the bouncers. Inside, I watched bleached media babes making heterosexual eyes at younger ebony-skinned rough trade. By the time I'd finished a pint I'd had enough. I crossed Old Street then cut down Great Eastern Street to Bethnal Green Road. I stood on the corner with Club Row soliciting business. I didn't want to go home alone. I wanted company that would pay its own way. I wanted to turn a trick. Pussy darling?

A twenty-something looked bashfully at me. Come on. I beckoned him with my finger. Offered verbal encouragement. Come on. He was embarrassed. Shy. Stammered. He wanted something rather unusual. I assured him I'd done it all. Oral. Anal. Three-in-a-bed. He couldn't shock me. He asked the price for straight sex. I told him. He wanted to know if I'd read something aloud for the same money. He promised me it wouldn't take more than five minutes. I agreed. Positioned myself under a lamp post. He fumbled in his pocket, eventually pulling out a sheet of paper.

I slowly read through the text. A first person narrative about a prostitute and a john who go down to the canal at Kings Cross. While the punter is getting a blow job, he notices what he takes to be a body in the water. The oral is abandoned and they haul what is actually a plastic dummy in a skimpy dress and long blonde wig onto the canal bank. A hole has been drilled between its legs and filled with raw mince. A discussion ensues and they conclude a pervert has been getting his kicks by fucking the mannequin.

Upon reaching the end of this piece, I handed it back to the john. He asked if I found it shocking. When I replied in the negative, he expressed surprise that I wasn't curious to know what happened next. I told him his name and revealed my familiarity with the narrative. The punter dismissed the prostitute and had sex with the dummy. Alfred Cain may not have been a household name, but he was highly regarded by the art world. This work-in-progress – which entailed surreptitiously recording prostitutes reading perverse tales – had already been previewed in Digital Arts News.

Cain was impressed and praised me lavishly as a tart with her fingers on the pulse of contemporary culture. I decided to play along with these fantasies, a strategy which enabled me to persuade Alfie that until he'd paid me to service him sexually, his audio project was just so much art wank. We bought filled bagels on Brick Lane and then retired to Cain's pad on Cheshire Street. The first thing I noticed inside his flat was a shelf full of Ripper books. I decided to do the business and then quiz the john about his true crime obsessions.

To excite Cain, who was not particularly attractive, I told him that prior to modernism it was the rule that in art all should be in good proportion and form a pleasing unity, whereas in lust the reverse was true. Carnality was fed by depravity, incongruity and perversity. Tall men took particular pleasure in coupling with dwarfs. The old lecher's senile passion was stimulated by immature girls. Elderly matrons took boys of sixteen in their arms. Now all that was changed, great art was ugly and age had been abolished by the maturation of the commodity form, which infantilised everybody.

Inflamed by these words, Alfie dropped his pants and bid me feel the weight of his member. I cupped my palm beneath his willy and it rose with strong muscular jerks. Soon it stood proudly up by itself at a slight angle from his hairy belly. I curled my fingers around the shaft and felt it throb beneath my iron grip. Without letting go, I sat down in a chair and pulled Cain towards me. I ran my tongue along his length, then clamped my lips around it. With my head bobbing back and forth I quickly extracted his tribute.

Alfie made espresso. As he was busying himself, I asked about his Ripper obsession. He explained that he was making a film based on the Whitechapel murders. When he revealed that a Karl Marx lookalike was cast as the Ripper, I giggled. Alfie insisted that this prank would spring him out of the art ghetto. Right wing journalists were bound to fall for a hoax about Marx being a homicidal maniac and the liberal press would ridicule them for believing a man who died before the Ripper murders took place made a credible suspect. Cain was anticipating a publicity bonanza.

I asked Cain his opinions about Henry James as a Jack the Ripper suspect and he laughed. Nevertheless, my hair stood on end when he insisted that James had been eliminated as a suspect way back in 1888. The story Cain related was that Thomas Ede appeared at the inquiry into the murder of Mary Ann Nichols, stating that he'd seen a suspicious looking man. Ede returned some days later declaring that he'd discovered his suspect was Henry James, an innocuous simpleton. After some banter back and forth, we realised we were talking about different men with the same name.

However, I immediately realised I could make something of this coincidence. Henry James the novelist might have disguised himself as a madman with a wooden arm and hired lodgings in the East End in order to carry out the Ripper murders. Using his real name was a double bluff, since he was far too respectable for anyone to make innuendoes about what he got up to sexually with tailor's dummies. The chief literary suspect for the Ripper crimes was George Gissing, who'd lost his college scholarship after turning to crime to keep his prostitute mistress in booze. He got caught.

I told Alfie about Adam Scald and he dismissed as silly the notion that James Boswell had founded a secret society for literary men who wished to murder and mutilate prostitutes. That said, Cain was impressed by the notion that a working class lorry driver had been fitted up for the Yorkshire Ripper slayings when the culprit was actually the literary hack Bruce Chatwin. Boswell's posthumous fame was secure and he didn't require this type of PR campaign – but Chatwin's books were tiresome and this was just the thing to fan flagging interest. Indeed, it was a publicist's wet dream

Alfie didn't know anything about Henry James but his flatmate – literary reviewer Alex Clerk – owned most of the master's works as well as several biographies. Alexander was on vacation, so we went through to his room and hit a literary goldmine. Cain flicked through a Philip Horne introduction to the OUP edition of *A London Life* and *The Reverberator*, featuring a negative assessment of WT Stead's journalistic exploitation of prostitution under the sensational headline 'The Maiden Tribute Of Modern Babylon'. This plugged us straight into fresh speculations, since several Ripperologists uncritically utilised Stead as an expert on Victorian vice.

James and his friend Edmund Gosse viewed Stead's journalistic japes – for example, procuring a London virgin and personally transporting her abroad to illustrate the mechanics of "the white slave trade" – as infinitely discouraging. In *The Reverberator*, James attacked the ways in which the press lowered intellectual and moral standards. Cain and I surmised that, disappointed by the lack of response to his ruminations on scandal in *A London Life* and *The Reverberator* as they appeared serially in 1888, James embarked on the Jack the Ripper murders to prove that recourse to depravity generated extensive, salacious and morally ambiguous newspaper coverage.

This ambiguous utilisation of the press is reflected – at a lower pitch – both in the fiction Henry James produced and his other sojourns amongst prostitutes. Our conjectures took on the colouring of fact as we examined *The Complete Notebooks Of Henry James,* edited by Leon Edel and Lyall H. Powers (OUP 1987). The only dated entries for 1888 were inscribed 5 January and 11 March. Lyndall Gordon in *A Private Life Of Henry James: Two Women and His Art* talked about the writer's friends losing sight of his movements in the latter part of 1888 and of him ultimately vanishing.

Where Gordon miscalculated was by assuming that James sought to create a smokescreen around his intimate relations with Constance Fenimore Woolson. The bluestocking was merely an effect James put in place to deflect attention from his real movements. It is telling that all the Ripper murders took place on weekends when James might fake an absence from London by writing letters in which he pretended he'd attended country house parties. Meanwhile, James was roughing it in a hovel he'd rented in Whitechapel, audaciously living under his own name while brazenly hamming it up as a lunatic with a wooden arm.

At the close of her book, Gordon writes of a terminally-ill James devoting a week to burning papers he did not wish anyone else to see. These must necessarily include the lost diary of Jack the Ripper, the missing James notebooks of 1888. Clearly, the work attributed to James Maybrick and published in 1993 as *The Diary Of Jack the Ripper* was a fake. In 1915 James destroyed the journals describing his activities as Jack the Ripper – alongside details of how he'd poisoned nine prostitutes in Paris and unleashed a fatal psychic attack on his invalid sister Alice James.

Returning to Alex Clerk's bookshelves, I found a useful selection of letters between James and his brother William published by The University Press of Virginia. In this there was a letter from Henry dated 19 January 1889 that contained statements about a visit to Alice which didn't quite tally with what he'd written to Boott the day before. Unfortunately, the volume threw little light on Henry's involvement in the murder of psychic investigator Edmund Gurney, so I turned my

attention to the academic peregrinations of Eve
Kosovsky Sedgwick – 'The Beast In The Closet: James
and the Writing of Homosexual Panic'.

I didn't find it mysterious that James had failed to
complete the volume of his memoirs that was to have
covered the Ripper murders. However, it took some
serious discussion over cold beers to elucidate how and
why James had exercised such influence over the upper
echelons of the British establishment. We decided that
each of the Ripper victims had been involved in blackmail attempts against establishment figures. I was too
tired and emotional to read through further books, so
Cain agreed that having come up with the broad outlines of our theory, we could fill in the details later.

By this time, Alfie was goat drunk, and once he'd
pressed a score into my palm I allowed him to wrench
off my clothes. Having exposed my quim to his eager
view, the hunchback – for Cain was assuredly a hunchback – sunk to his knees and mucilaged his lips to my
spur. I felt his spicy tongue lapping down there and
considered it prudent to suppress a giggle as several different representations of yapping poodles flashed
through my mind. Despite my feigning a shiver to sim-
ulate the climax of sexual conveyance, the engrossed
gimp continued in his artifice with evident relish.

After what seemed an eternity – I was eager to return to the more satisfying employment of slandering Henry James – the raspberry pushed me to my knees and, after clambering upon a footstool, pressed his protuberance into my moist breach. His sceptre was so much rancid spume. I might have clasped this shank but there was nothing to grab once his two inches disappeared into my upper cleft. I inhaled and the cripple writhed spasmodically. I tickled his perforation with my lingua and Cain's spastic limbs flailed helplessly. I felt a few slippery drops of fortitude on my tongue. He'd come.

James instrumentalised the slippages of language in burnished prose. With his international theme, James wanted to project himself as having mastered two sets of manners and simultaneously risen above both through this single act of sovereignty. Depending on the potential benefits, James might present himself as either aristocratic or an advocate of capitalism as a practical religion of money worship. However, this pose unravels as soon as one understands that James thought it was money which enabled him to be aristocratic. The clutching James singularly failed to grasp what it meant to belong to the aristocracy, let alone the proletariat.

To say that James was a bourgeois with aristocratic pretensions is to say that he was a man who had little to no understanding of his own – or, indeed, any other – time. In short, and leaving aside the issues raised by the fact that time itself is an epistemologically questionable construct, he was a reactionary. It therefore comes as no surprise that James subscribed to the romantic cult of Napoleon and that his admiration for the little corporal was premised on all the usual claptrap about the Will that attained its apotheosis in the pathetic dribblings of Friedrich Nietzsche.

Cain agreed when I suggested that James had the psychological profile of a serial killer. Projecting an image of toughness and success, he was – beneath this almost credible exterior – a seething mass of unresolved contradictions. While presenting himself to the world – through lessons to his disciples – as "the master", James suffered from a terrible lack of confidence. He was unable to tell right from wrong. He resented the massive book sales of critically unacclaimed writers. James was driven to kill and kill again to bolster his sense of self, which was constantly disintegrating. Henry James was, unarguably, Jack the Ripper.

Alfie suggested that this profile fitted George

Gissing just as well as James. Gissing eventually married Nell, the alcoholic prostitute who became his mistress. After Nell's death, Gissing luxuriated in the misery of a marriage to Edith, a slightly more respectable working class girl. Gissing had left England around the same time as Henry James fled Whitechapel. This was more than a coincidence. I decided Gissing was responsible for the murders of Emma Elizabeth Smith on 3 April 1888 and Martha Tabram on 7 August 1888. Way back when these murders were considered to be the work of the Ripper.

James, we agreed, was responsible for the next five murders, the slayings still popularly attributed to Jack the Ripper. I figured that what we needed was another literary figure to finger for the slayings of Rose Mylett on 20 December 1888, Alice McKenzie on 17 July 1889, the unidentified female torso found on 10 September 1889 and Frances Coles on 13 February 1891. All assumed to be prostitutes. Cain suggested Baron Corvo. I vetoed this idea not simply on the grounds that Rolfe was too obscure – but because Gissing would inevitably become the central mediating figure between him and James.

All three of these writers were political reactionaries, but Gissing and Corvo gave themselves more freely to fictionalised wish-fulfilment and pseudo-autobiography. James had a greater imaginative faculty than the other two men, as well as being a superior prose stylist. Returning to Gissing, Samuel Vogt Garp concluded after extensive study that the novelist's reactionary views arose from his training as a classicist. Garp believed that reading the classics often produced a conservative outlook. This argument can be extended; conventional novels clearly cause timid minds to reproduce themselves as centred subjects. Novels are the cultural spew of the bourgeoisie.

Alfie nominated William Burroughs our third man. Beat writer converted orgone accumulator into a time machine. Travelled to Victorian Whitechapel and killed cunt. Burroughs well known for his misogyny. Gap of seventeen months between penultimate and last slaying of 13 February 1891 due to miscalculation when duration blaster settings adjusted. Wrong day. No massacre. No good. *No bueno*. Sterling mutilations fried before his peepers. Cut through lines time and space. Died yesterday. Asseverations plunging. Representations plunging. Fracture in flat chamber. Sirocco the effervescence study. Cabotinage. Most putrescent pieces habitually stood quiescent before death. Saucy Jack writing from hell. Mister Lusk.

Despite these slippages my narrative refused to break down. Literary cops everywhere. Burroughs reminded me of Gissing. Both writers fatalistically fell into unbearable domestic situations. Gissing with Marianne Helen Harrison and Edith Underwood. Burroughs with the Ian Sommerville and Miss Alan Watson menage-a-trois in Dover Street. Both writers were politically conservative but found themselves incapable of living conventional lives. Neither wrote well, but concern with technical innovation forced Burroughs into confrontation with bourgeois values. Quantity and quality. Form transforming content. Burroughs juxtaposed with Angus Wilson claiming Ivy Compton-Burnett pointed the way forward at 1962 Edinburgh writers conference.

Burroughs and Gissing lived the low-life – not in actuality but as a fiction. Burroughs was an agent of chaos and control. In pulling the old con cop tough cop routine, he'd transformed two roles into one. Schizophrenic theatre. Despite his best efforts, Burroughs heroically failed to constitute himself as a centred subject. Gissing had more to recommend him as a Ripper suspect – but there were fewer reasons to read his books. As a writer, Gissing's only virtue was that he gave prostitutes a more prominent place in novels such as The Unclassed than was the norm in Victorian literature.

Cain mentioned James Maybrick and I laughed. The alleged author of *The Diary of Jack The Ripper* had nothing to commend him. Far more damning than the lack of any evidence to prove this document genuine was its content. A failed attempt at combining poetry and prose. A complete bummer from beginning to end. Not worth reading. Even the publishers must have considered it trash, since they prefaced the diary with two hundred pages of generously spaced bilge about the Whitechapel murders. I told Alfie to forget Maybrick and Burroughs. We would attribute the post-Kelly slayings to Samuel Butler.

Cain then countered that William Burroughs was a prime Ripper suspect. Many recent writers have suggested the Ripper killings were Masonic rituals and Cain made much of the fact this beat novelist had lived in Duke Street, which houses the Supreme Council of orthodox Masonry. I wasn't impressed, and retorted that Henry James had lived in the same street as JK Stephen at the time of the murders. I did not for a minute believe that the Ripper was a Mason. The killings were orchestrated by various literary men who wished to extricate themselves from scandals involving East End prostitutes.

Cain had read *Jack the Ripper Revealed* by John Wilding and attempted to make something of the fact that Henry James made no appearance in it. Wilding fingered JK Stephen assisted by MJ Druitt. Naturally enough, I insisted that there were flaws in Wilding's argument. He took two letters and a piece of graffiti attributed to the Ripper and, in treating them both as anagrams, created messages in which Stephen indicted both himself and Druitt for the killings. However, even if Stephen was responsible for these messages, Wilding states that his suspect was insane, which means his testimony is inadmissible.

My solution was simple: Wilding correctly decoded the messages but they came from Henry James who hated JK Stephen. James knew Stephen and his parents – who were neighbours in De Vere Gardens – through the young man's uncle Leslie Stephen. JK Stephen had tutored Prince Albert Victor, and James, a dreadful snob, was envious of these royal connections. The youngster edited a literary and political magazine called *The Reflector* and this is lampooned in *The Reveberator*, a short novel written by James in 1887 and first published in 1888. The family owed James some serious favours, so this affront was overlooked.

Another link between Henry James and JK Stephen

was their recondite friendships with the life-long bachelor Arthur Christopher Benson, the eldest son of the Archbishop of Canterbury. JK Stephen befriended AR Benson in the 1870s when both men were pupils at Eton. Henry James was nearly two decades older than Benson and they became intimate in the mid-1880s – prior to the Whitechapel murders. Around this time, Benson was teaching at Eton. He eventually became an independent man of letters. Benson shared with James top-drawer social and literary affiliations, plus a conception of life as ferocious and sinister.

In keeping with recent speculation about the Ripper, I decided to make Mary Kelly the central figure in my story. In the early 1880s, Kelly was living in Bassett Road – off Ladbroke Grove – where she'd been installed by Leslie Stephen as his mistress. Kelly came to London from Ireland via Wales and was a fresh-faced teenager. In 1882 she gave birth to a daughter, Virginia, who was taken from her and brought up in the Stephen household where she passed as legitimate fruit of her father's marriage. Virginia eventually got hitched to Leonard Woolf and became a successful novelist.

Kelly resented the baby being taken from her and fell out with Leslie Stephen. To keep her sweet, he had to provide a paramour, and Henry James was brought in to do the requisite plumbing. This relationship lasted until Kelly became pregnant. James was single and Kelly was promised the baby. However, her son was cruelly snatched away from her and brought up as Roger Fry. He eventually became a leading member of the Bloomsbury Group. Kelly fled to the East End where she worked as a prostitute. Her clients included the literary agent AP Watt, who got her pregnant.

At this point, Kelly hatched her plot to blackmail the various upper class literary beaus who had got her up the duff. Kelly was one of several prostitutes who were sickened by their exploitation at the hands of literary blades and decided that having paid for sex, these swains would also shell out for silence about their peccadilloes. George Gissing pulled the first two jobs on behalf of Wilkie Collins. The impecunious Gissing was paid off both with better book deals and, eventually, representation by AP Watt. Having previously married the courtesan Nell, Gissing greatly enjoyed snuffing two cockney streetwalkers.

Henry James took greater pleasure in butchering bawds than the masochistic Gissing did in taking one as his wife. Needless to say, James was also fond of killing cats. The first four hits James discharged were favours for various figures including Robert Bridges,

Robert Browning, Richard Burton, Thomas Hardy, George Meredith and Alfred Tennyson. Roughing it with East End whores became a craze among Victorian literary gentlemen, so many of these concubines were blackmailing more than one gallant. The theatrical nature of the Whitechapel murders was designed not simply to indulge the Ripper's sexual solecisms, but also to discourage crossbiting.

Disposing of Kelly proved more delicate for James than ripping his earlier victims. AP Watt wanted his unborn child to live, so Kelly was abducted and another victim mutilated in her place. Kelly wasn't murdered until she'd given birth in 1889. Her third child was switched with a still-born baby and grew up to be the literary critic John Middleton Murray. And so since Kelly had been his consort, James was careful to establish a smoke screen around his movements throughout November 1888. His biographer Fred Kaplan admits that James gave conflicting information concerning his whereabouts to different parties.

Henry James was better rewarded for his efforts than George Gissing – but then they were more spectacular than anything an individual hailing from the lower-middle classes was likely to achieve. James had placed his professional concerns in the care of AP Watt at the beginning of 1888. Hearing this, Kelly approached the literary agent claiming to be a friend of the novelist and quickly became embroiled with his representative. James felt partially responsible when Kelly attempted to blackmail Watt. He was, however, well reward for sorting this and other matters out. 1888 was one of his best years financially.

Cain complained that my solution was too esoteric for the average punter and that they'd prefer the theory, put forward by Melvyn Fairclough in *The Ripper & The Royals,* that Lord Randolph Churchill was the leader of the gang responsible for the Whitechapel murders. I dissed Fairclough for his dependence on a bunch of dodgy diaries with no provenance and even less literary merit. Alfie insisted that books such as those by Fairclough, Wilding and Stephen Knight had damaged the royal family. I agreed, but made it clear that I found Sir William Gull and John Netley too tiresome to discuss.

As we spoke, William Burroughs materialised before our incredulous peepers. The controls of his temporality blaster had malfunctioned. As the beat writer dissembled himself, Alfie grabbed him by the right arm, while I caught hold of his left coat sleeve. The room shimmered and soon was no more. Where once four walls had surrounded us, there was nothing but foul night air. We were in Whitechapel at a time when it had theatres and music halls with cheap rates of admission that served to absorb local residents – who thus found themselves both royally entertained and kept out of harm's way.

The Earl of Effingham, a theatre in Whitechapel Road, had recently been done up and restored. It held three thousand people but had no boxes. Whitechapel did not go out in kid-gloves and white ties. The stage was very roomy, and the trapwork extensive; Whitechapel rejoiced in pyrotechnic displays, blue demons, red demons and vanishing Satans that disappeared in a cloud of smoke through an invisible hole in the floor. Great was the applause when gauzy nymphs rose like so many Aphrodites from the sea, and sat down on fake sunbeams midway between the stage and a theatrical heaven.

The Pavilion theatre stood close by the Earl of Effingham. On approaching the playhouse, I observed prostitutes gathered outside in little gangs and knots of three or four. When they ventured inside, it was usually in company with their men. Many of the prostitutes had ongoing relationships with sailors that would be picked up whenever their man came back onshore –

and continue until the money accumulated while away at sea ran out. The Eastern Music Hall boasted a gallery set aside for sailors and their women, so that tradesmen might enjoy performances unmolested by those who revelled in drunken fights.

Another concert hall, the British Queen in Commercial Road, was much frequented by whores. As we approached it, two hookers were arrested for attempting to murder a man. The face of one was heavy and repulsive, her forehead low and her nose short with dilated nostrils. The other was much better looking. When we got inside the British Queen, it was filled with brazen-faced women, dressed in gaudy colours, pirouetting in a fantastic manner. The quick-time shrill of flutes and a fiddle combined with the braying of the trumpet to rouse those present to waltz with great velocity.

Perhaps I'm biased, but I noted something prepossessing about the faces of the whores – which is more than could be said of their johns. They showed a compound of resignation, indifference and recklessness, all phases through which any prostitute must pass in the course of her ill-esteemed career. A harlot is not thoroughly inured to her vocation until she has experienced them all and they have become mingled together. There is a delicacy about a woman metering her twat. She is determined to unite business and pleasure within the limitations of circumstances that many would find impossible to endure.

The faces of the johns I observed after the temporality blaster took us back to 1888 were vacant, stupid and drunk. We entered a brothel in Frederick Street, then proceeded to Brunswick Street, both locations notorious for their bordellos and thieves' lodging houses. The rooms in the whore-houses were relatively spacious and boasted four-poster beds, several of which were decked out with dirty, faded chintz curtains. The mantelpieces over fireplaces were decorated with cheap crockery. Rosewood or gilt-framed mirrors surmounted them. Burroughs was showing us whores a cut above his prey; the street was his stalking ground.

As we followed him on his hellish mission, it became apparent that he subscribed to the use of rites, ceremonies, adjurations and incantations to a powerful and personal spirit of evil, whose favour he intended to obtain by means of orgies that for horror, blasphemy and obscenity must exceed all that had proceeded them. Burroughs believed that, as a necromancer, he had to outrage and degrade human nature in every conceivable way. The very least of crimes necessary to obtain the power he craved was ritual murder, and the more degraded the unwilling victim chosen for the sacrifice the better.

The black magic Burroughs practised employed the agencies of evil spirits and demons. The substances required for success in this field included strips of skin from a suicide, nails from a gallows, candles made from human fat, the head of a black cat which had been fed for forty days on human flesh, the horns of a goat that had been buggered by a man, and a preparation made from the uterus of a harlot. Burroughs despatched his first four victims on a cross, a typically Satanic inversion. He'd buggered his victims and slit their throats while taking this pleasure.

If only Jack the Ripper investigators had entered time travel into their equations, then the identity of the killer would have been known long ago. Most Ripperologists simply used the Whitechapel Murders as a focus for their own hallucinations, rather than investigating the crimes objectively and with an open mind. Burroughs wanted me to know the truth, so that I could break through the tissue of lies that surrounded his career as a highly successful black magician. This work performed, Burroughs sent us back to Alfie's room in my present time. The walls shimmering, wobbling, but solid to my touch.

As Cain and I sobered up with some oral sex, we somehow hit upon the idea of breaking into Adam Scald's house on Fournier Street. I'd lifted Adam's wallet, so we knew the address. I was hoping to get my hands on evidence that would prove Scald was a cold-blooded killer, driven to mutilating prostitutes by an insane but unshakeable conviction he'd been Jack the Ripper in a previous life. Up to this point in the paragraph we'd been head to toe, mouth to groin, but we disentangled our bodies, dressed and hurried out of the swank yuppie flat.

Making our way down Brick Lane, we saw on the corner of Hanbury Street various members of the feminist art group Ball Busters Unlimited videoing kerb-crawlers. They would name and shame the johns concerned. We passed on, took a right at the next turn. Scald's house had been ransacked. The door stood open. Smashed furniture and torn papers littered the ground floor. We didn't bother checking out the upstairs rooms. We wended back up Brick Lane. There was a commotion going on in Hanbury Street. We approached it and saw Scald lying dead, mutilated, at an original Ripper site.

Amy appeared without warning and drew me aside to explain everything and nothing. She wasn't really a crack hoe, that was just her cover story, she was actually a marketing consultant who'd been paid to draw gullible trippers into the East End. She'd figured that if murdered prostitutes could be transformed into a money-spinner, then cutting up a few of the men who paid for sex would serve to increase the lucrative trade generated by the Ripper trail. Amy wanted to diversify the appeal of the murder sites by adding a feminist frisson. Lesbian separatists had to dig it.

I allowed Amy to lead Alfie Cain off for a steamy session at the Dorset Street murder site. I liked Alfie, and, if he was to die, I didn't want to feel in any way responsible. Time had flown by. I'd enjoyed myself with Alfie. But I had an appointment with the cast and crew of a snuff movie which I intended to keep. I needed a man, or rather a victim. Alan Abel picked me up on Quaker Street. I told him he could have free sex as long as he didn't mind being filmed screwing several different girls.

Alan was delighted by my proposition and said he'd like to fuck me first. He must have thought I was vain. Seeing him squirming beneath me as he croaked was a more attractive proposition. I steered Abel into the basement of the brothel. Alan stripped off and lay naked on the couch that had been provided for his pleasure. I rolled a condom down his length and he groaned appreciatively. We got it on and it went on and on. Alan eventually complained that I wouldn't let him come. The cameras kept rolling as I drunkenly explained the money shot.

After I'd strutted my stuff, I was replaced by Jean Smith, a dainty little thing of seventy-two, quite a treat for those who like older women. I'm told she gives a demon blow job when she takes her false teeth out. Alan attempted to get up and go. I told him to smile sweetly, after reminding him of our deal. Since he was getting free sex, he had to take what came and couldn't pick or choose. A bodyguard called Wolf laughed viciously and cracked his knuckles. Abel wasn't enjoying himself but he put a brave face on things.

When Jean had finished with Alan, Wolf got the old lady to take out her false teeth and give him a blow job. As a gangster, he thought this showed class. Meanwhile, Abel was getting it from Karen Eliot, a big buxom woman with an artistic bent. All Karen's fingers were painted with different colours of nail varnish. Karen made Alan give her a shrimp job and then fiddled about with his dick. Since Karen is only forty and has nice bleached blonde hair, Abel gave as good as he got. Karen gave him a lick, he licked her out.

At nineteen, Brenda George was the youngest fuck Alan was going to get. Brenda had already been seen all over town in the best of company – sportsmen, pop singers and notorious criminals. This demimonde appreciated the way she got her tits out whenever flash-bulbs began to pop. If the press wasn't about then classy Brenda found the popping of champagne corks a most satisfactory substitute. George got on top of Abel and ground her way down to the base of his prick. While she kept him stiff, the girls yelled at Alan to chew the ends of her long hair.

After this feast of split-ends, Abel got a dark-haired treat in the form of Angela Malakoff. A truly tasty dish, Angela could hardly speak English, but I'm assured she's a regular scrabble player in her native Russian. The mafia organised the complicated travel arrangements that saw her arriving in London via Finland, Sweden and Denmark. Five years on, Malakoff was still paying off her mafia debt. Angela liked anal sex because she got paid extra for it. Her arse was well stretched and rarely bled, even when her male partner was as unskilled a plumber as Alan Abel.

Susan Lamb came next and since she'd just been to

the clap clinic for a diagnosis and had yet to undergo a cure, she used a rubber. Not that Susan was worried about Alan catching the pox, her concern was solely for the hoes who'd follow her heavyweight act. Lamb was a big girl, so big that when she sat on top of a man he was rendered helpless. As Susan bounced up and down above Abel, I could hear our star gasping for breath. Lamb faked an orgasm, all the while taking great pains to ensure Alan didn't come.

Fiona Jones had little going for her other than being the same age as Jesus when he died, thirty-three. Fiona was plain with a foul temper and a permanent frown. She made little effort to show herself off to any advantage, avoiding make-up and dressing in cheap frumpy clothes bought off-the-peg. While Jones wasn't shrewd, neither was she so stupid that she didn't realise most of the men who fucked her were blind drunk and it mattered little to them what she looked like. They were merely looking for a hole in which to relieve themselves.

Sharon Peters was a real broken doll. She had a limp, a squint and a finger missing from her left hand. I'm told she had once been young and pretty, but two years of crack addiction took her little girl charms and her pimp thought his merchandise so badly spoilt that severing a finger made little difference. Sharon was just twenty-one but looked at least forty. She provided a living, breathing, shambling warning against the dangers of drug abuse. Peters was barely aware of what she was doing, and I had to remind her not to make Alan come.

Mary Thatcher was an alcoholic. I'd not noticed the open sores on her backside before and wondered how they'd got there. We were making a sleazy snuff movie so these features weren't a problem. I could see Mary wasn't getting the better paid type of work any longer. She'd had a drink problem for the best part of ten years and at twenty-seven she was too far gone in this degeneracy to reclaim either her looks or her sanity. I've heard that these days she hangs about outside pubs, since kerb-crawlers are generally too sober to touch her.

Margaret Whitehouse was an escaped lunatic, much given to bouts of howling. Generally this wasn't a problem if it occurred during sex, since johns would interpret it as a sign of their sexual prowess. Punters tended to find Margaret's claim that she was the Virgin Mary more worrying, but fortunately she rarely alluded to this belief unless the moon was full in the sky. Although Whitehouse was a fully-grown woman of thirty-eight, I'd been told by a psychiatrist that she needs to be watched over constantly. She had attempted to kill herself on at least twenty-six occasions.

Joy Brown was a speed freak. She fucked Alan and simultaneously discoursed about the holocaust against native Americans carried out by Spanish conquistador Francisco Pizarro. Unable to win battles against superior armaments, the Inca King Atahaulpa arranged a meeting with Pizarro in the town of Cajamarca. However, instead of cutting a deal, Pizarro slaughtered seven thousand native Americans and imprisoned Atahaulpa. The Inca King paid a ransom for his freedom by filling a large room with gold, silver and precious stones. Then, instead, of being freed, Atahaulpa was forcibly converted to Christianity and once he'd been baptised, was immediately killed.

Rachel McCory believed the British royal family were reptiles who'd assumed human form, but that during ritual sacrifices they reverted to type and ate their victims alive. Knowing Rachel had become addicted to smack after getting into drugs through reading William Burroughs books, I didn't take her very seriously. Like most prostitutes, she was a sex worker for the money and if she ever shook off her habit, she'd probably take up some other line of work. Rachel didn't look like she enjoyed fucking Alan, but then she didn't seem to enjoy anything other than getting out of her tree.

Sarah Becker had turned to prostitution in order to support her two kids. What interested her was getting money out of johns. Watching her fuck Alan, I could see that her approach was perfunctory. Sarah was a level-headed girl, not the type to buy into conspiracy theories, so I was surprised to learn that she believed Princess Diana had been murdered by British intelligence to avert a constitutional crisis. But then, Sarah was Diana mad. She'd long been in the habit of adopting the clothes and hairstyles popularised by the princess, and so attracted a peculiar type of john.

Louise Lincoln didn't want to fuck Alan at all. She complained he was a pig. He'd paid her for sex a few days before and couldn't stop farting as they did the business. Louise was temperamental but all it took was for Wolf to crack his knuckles and she saw the error of her ways. Lincoln couldn't afford to pick and choose her clients. She was pimped by her boyfriend, an exceptionally violent young man who often beat her up. Had Louise only been wiser in her choice of lovers, she wouldn't have found herself on the street turning tricks.

Anne Bundi was every john's fantasy, a true devotee of the goddess Venus, a veritable nymphomaniac. Bundi was sensuous and vain. Why, if it wasn't for her pride, she wouldn't charge for sex. Anne loved her work, which she viewed as a pleasure. She liked to lie back and let any man prepared to place a score in her palm have his way with her. Anne didn't notice Alan was looking extremely dishevelled. She liked the attention her work brought her and wasn't fussy about where such considerations came from. I've heard that many of her best friends are cops.

Samantha Bissett believed she was the reincarnation of the assassinated Roman emperor Lucius Domitius Aurelianus and that every time she had an orgasm she relived his death, screaming at the height of her passion about being betrayed by her own officers. Alan wasn't interested in Samantha's story of a common soldier rising through the ranks and eventually being elected to imperial power. Samantha clearly despised Alan and her performance was crassly hammed up. When she faked her orgasm, she sounded more like a pregnant cow being aborted than a woman in the full throws of ecstasy. *Quis custodes custodiet ipsos.*

Charlotte Meyer had a fine pair of lungs. She'd never had a pimp, although she'd once been married, and it's said that the whole of Bethnal Green was disturbed when this shrew scolded her husband. Her spouse left eventually, although whether on his own two feet or in a coffin, I'm not sure. The maenad would have made a fine dominatrix if she'd been a little more sophisticated. Instead our termagant worked Wentworth Street and often frightened johns into paying over the odds for her dubious charms. There was little danger of Alan falling asleep while Charlotte was upbraiding him.

Polly Jackson had two great assets, an enormous pair of knockers. She got Alan to bury his face in them. Her usual trick was to get johns to give her a pearl necklace. However, in Alan's case she was under strict instructions not to let him come. So Polly gave Alan's prick a few licks, then took his todger all the way down her throat. It wasn't that Jackson was gagging for it, she simply wanted brass to fund her booze habit. This was a hit and run operation with Abel's pork sword being regurgitated before he shot his load.

Pauline Gates was bored of life. She took no pleasure from sucking cock but it was an easy way of earning money to pay for her crack. Pauline liked smoking rocks, she liked it so much that she couldn't think about anything else. Her eyes were blank, her face lined, her clothes tattered, her hair lank, her hands shook, she had a stoop and she limped. Gates was twenty-four years old and from the lazy way she worked Alan's cock with her teeth and her tongue you'd have thought she hadn't slept for twenty-four hours. Perhaps she hadn't.

Jasmine Philips was very much like Pauline Gates and Sharon Peters, a real broken doll with a limp and a stoop. She was prematurely aged from smoking rocks. She provided a living, breathing, shambling warning against the dangers of drug addiction. Jasmine was barely aware of what she was doing, and I had to remind her not to make Alan come. She wasn't thinking about her work, she wasn't thinking about the drugs she'd be able to buy with the money she was earning; she didn't think, period. Philips was a zombie hooker, twenty-two and getting on for dead.

After two consecutive bouts of sex with the living dead, Abel was treated to the epicurean Koonika Tradmata. A truly delightful lady, Koonika could barely speak English, but rest assured she's a regular brain-box in her native Estonian. The mafia organised the complicated travel arrangements that saw her arriving in London via Lithuania, Poland and Germany. Three years on, Tradmata was still paying off her mafia debt. Koonika liked anal sex because she got paid extra for it. Her arse was well stretched and rarely bled, even when her male partner was as unskilled a plumber as Alan Abel.

Daphne Rhodes was a runaway from an abusive father and inadequate mother, left behind somewhere in the north of England. Daphne had fled her family when she was fifteen. Having reached twenty, it had yet to sink in that, five years on, she was standing still rather than running. Daphne had everything that a john could desire – a mouth, two hands and a hole between her legs – plus much more to boot, like a lot of psychological problems. She gave Alan a wearied look and got on with the business in hand, keeping him excited but not letting him come.

The most notable thing about Lilith Austin was her teeth. More than one john has recited his fantasies about finding a similar set while plumbing Lilith's cunt. Austin doesn't need to blow her own trumpet, she just sucks men on the horn. This entails less effort and less wear than straight sex, and the act may be accomplished with ease in the street, which is why so many whores prefer it to missionary capers. There is also the little matter of trust. A man who places his plonker between the teeth of a harlot demonstrates his faith in our profession.

Sarah Smith boasted another fine set of teeth, so it was a shame about the rest of her. Heroin often makes men thin and causes women to bloat out, and this was certainly true in Sarah's case. She had curves in all the right places and many more to boot. Fortunately she knew what to do with her teeth and could make most punters come in a minute flat. Not that this skill was of any use while we were making a snuff movie of Alan Abel being fucked to death. Alan didn't come but Sarah made his cock bleed.

Mary Jones came next and since she'd just been to the clap clinic for a diagnosis and had yet to undergo a cure, she used a rubber. Susan was plain with a foul temper and a permanent frown. She provided a living, breathing, shambling warning against the dangers of drug addiction. Peters was barely aware of what she was doing, and I had to remind her not to make Alan come. I could see Sarah wasn't getting the better paid type of work any longer. But I hear she gives a demon blow job when her false teeth are out.

Simone de Beauvoir was a real gone chick. She talked about the myth of woman in five authors as she fucked. She wasn't speeding and she could converse until she was blue in the face while simultaneously making the most conservative punters forgive her French. Actually, a lot of johns wanted french, so it was a shame Simone hadn't mastered the art of discoursing while sucking cock. By this time, Alan was beginning to suspect he'd got the bad side of a poor bargain, but I didn't care since Wolf would deal with Abel if he got out of hand.

Alan had already complained about not being allowed to come, and as these reproaches became increasingly shrill they began to get on my wick. He claimed he'd be able to get it up again within minutes of shooting his wad, but nobody believed him. So when Erica Gormley took Simone de Beauvoir's place, I went upstairs with the shockingly intellectual bluestocking prostitute who sold herself to many men in order to avoid being enslaved by one. I was not born a woman, I was forcibly transformed into one during my adolescence, de Beauvoir frequently fulminated about the curse afflicting her.

As I made coffee, Simone started banging on about the similarities between marriage and prostitution. She saw marriage as a long term contract with a single man to ensure the economic well-being of the woman, whereas prostitution consisted of numerous short term exchanges to secure the same end. I insisted that the quantity of these short term encounters transformed their quality but de Beauvoir would have none of it.

Her extremely simplistic reading of Hegel was derived in its entirety from Alexandre Kojève, whereas I'd started from Stace's equally reductive perspective but my understanding had broadened out from there.

Simone just couldn't see that the snuff movie we'd been making had been inspired by Hegel's exposition of the relationship between quantity and quality. Her analysis was closely related to those types of Marxist-Freudianism that had been popular in the 1960s and early '70s, until this type of speculation had disappeared almost without trace. Simone might have rejected the notion of penis envy, but she bought into too much of Freud to be taken seriously. Since I didn't care to engage with her melange of psychoanalysis, anthropology, literary criticism, pop philosophy and pseudo-Marxist existentialism, I decided to split.

I resolved to take a walk before heading back to our snuff movie set. There were guys in their pyjamas and dressing gowns, some of them looked like they were in their wives' dressing gowns, going into the storefront mosques along Redchurch Street. It was Ramadan, so the local Bengali men couldn't be bothered to dress when they got up for their extra early-morning worship. In any case, I guess a lot of them went back to bed afterwards. Moments later, I reached my flat, only to find the place wrecked with the front door wrenched off its hinges.

As I stood in the hall, Amy emerged from my bedroom. She told me a gentleman was paying way over the odds to hold a re-enactment of Mary Kelly's murder. My pad was the best location she could secure at short notice. I began to protest but Amy thrust a wad of bills in my hand. She said more dosh would follow and assured me the damage could be sorted out if I just stayed away for a couple of nights. I didn't want to pass up the wedge, but I wouldn't abandon my flat without some further reassurances.

Amy could see I was in two minds about what to do, so she dragged me out onto the stairwell. What she told me was well sick, but then since I'd started turning tricks I'd learnt that a john might seem alright the first couple of times he fucked you, but it wouldn't be long before the pervert wanted to pay for some deviation his wife found absolutely nauseating. Since pricks paid extra for weirdness, I was quite happy to indulge them – but a lot of the common prostitutes I'd met preferred to avoid the more depraved type of client.

The guy Amy had in my flat was both wealthy and mentally unstable. In his mind Mary Kelly the Ripper victim and Mary Kelly the feminist artist were the same person. Edward Kelly had somehow convinced himself not only that he was the son of the installation artist Mary Kelly, but that he was the scryer of the Elizabethan magus John Dee. Edward felt he'd been exploited by his pseudo-mother when she'd made the 'Post-Partum Document' about the first five years of her son's life, so he'd killed her as the climax to his Jack the Ripper butchery.

Edward was at least ten years too old to be Mary Kelly's son, but he was as outraged by her work as the tabloids had been when she'd exhibited soiled nappies at the Institute of Contemporary Arts way back in 1976. However, what sickened Edward was not so much that his crap should be exhibited as art, but that his mother should so cynically exploit their relationship to push her cod-Lacanian psychobabble. Edward was enraged that the woman he Oedipally misidentified should buy into Freudian bullshit about the baby being the mother's substitute phallus. Edward couldn't abide psychoanalytic theory.

To get his own back on his non-mother, artist Mary Kelly, for exploiting and humiliating him to build her gallery career, Edward compulsively acted out the death of the artificer by repeatedly restaging the death of the last Ripper victim Mary Kelly. Being rich,

Edward could afford to pay way over the odds to hire the homes of feminist artists, while also employing a few whores to look on as he smashed the arty pads to pieces, then ripped apart a life-size replica of a woman made out of papermaché he'd spent weeks constructing specifically for this purpose.

Edward Kelly was clearly traumatised by some childhood experience and, since money was a universal medium of exchange, I accepted the financial inducements offered for the destruction of my flat. The place was already wrecked and all that remained to be acted out was a ritual disembowelment, so I decided the best thing to do was split. However, before making my escape, I warned Amy that it was obvious her john was a retard who compensated for his immaturity by identifying with the image of Jack the Ripper – and because the identification was complete, he would soon turn to murder.

As I made my way across Bethnal Green Road I was thinking about Mary Kelly describing collections of baby memorabilia as a form of pornography for mothers. Despite the psychological clap-trap Kelly spewed, she'd really hit the mark with this observation, capturing the way patriarchy and capitalism stratify society with a shameless instrumentalisation of identity and difference. I was deep in these thoughts when I was accosted by a john. He wanted french and placed twenty knicker in my hand. As I blew him, Tom moaned about how going with high class hookers up west didn't satisfy his lusts.

Tom preferred honest East End tarts because, in his opinion, they were real. As he said this, my famous punter got all excited and came in my mouth. Once I'd spat Tom's spunk into the gutter, he offered me two score to accompany him to a party. I wasn't in a hurry to get back to the interminable snuff movie I'd set up, so I accepted the loot and followed the celebrity to a house on Wilkes Street. There were tiger skins on the floor and expensive post-modern art works on the walls. It was strictly wine, no beer.

Tom got drunk and started fumbling with my bra. I don't mind guys getting my tits out in front of their friends, but the deal I'd struck with my famous date was strictly bargain basement and didn't cover this exhibitionist service. I started screaming Tom's name and accusing him of being a cheap-skate. A television personality ought to pay more than a score for a blow job. The beautiful people present were embarrassed. They had a whip-round for their tight-fisted friend and ejected me from the party with a going away present of more than five ponies.

As I walked away from the house, I was followed. I didn't bother turning around. For some reason I assumed my pursuer was Tom. I heard running footsteps, felt a hand on my shoulder and when I spun around received an unpleasant surprise. I was confronted by a sleazeball who announced he was a journalist. He thought I'd like to sell my story to a tabloid newspaper. His editor would pay serious money and all he wanted to set this thing up was a free shag. I told him to fuck off, so he thrust his wallet in my hands.

The hack was plastered, so I took a twenty and gave the wallet back to him. We fell into a doorway and while the journalist fumbled with my dress, I thrust my knee hard against his groin. He doubled up, so I clasped my hands together and smashed them against his neck. The john went down and stayed down. I lifted his wallet, his watch, his gold cufflinks and tie clip. I tried the speed dialling function on his mobile. I woke the geezer's wife and told her he'd passed out drunk while I was fucking him in the street.

I walked off down the road. Once I'd turned into Brick Lane a taxi driver drew up and asked me if I'd like to be taken for a ride. I told him to cough up the readies if he wanted sex. The bloke said he cut up whores and he'd rip me apart if I stepped inside his cab. I still had the mobile in my hand, so I dialled the speaking clock in Australia and the cabbie looked confused as I held the phone against his ear. Then I threw the mobile against a wall and tottered off laughing.

Brick Lane is a one-way street and I was walking against the flow of traffic. The taxi driver must have parked his cab because he came charging down the road on foot, heading straight for me. I lifted up my petticoats and ran as best I could. I turned a couple of corners but I couldn't shake the bastard off. Luckily he was out of condition, so I was actually putting a little distance between us. The brothel loomed ahead and I shouted out for Fat Ron to open the door. Moments later, I flew breathlessly into the hallway.

The cabbie ran in behind me, and found himself instantly stopped by Fat Ron's fist. The bastard went down and, despite struggling to get up, he stayed down because Fat Ron's boots broke his jaw. Once the cabbie was unconscious, we stripped him naked and I got blood on my dress as we tied his hands behind his back. We walked back to Brick Lane and found his cab. Using the keys we'd appropriated, Ron started it up and we rode back to the brothel. We put the cabbie inside and after locating his address, drove to his Bow pad.

Fat Ron gave me the keys and I opened the door to the cabbie's terraced house. Ron carried my would-be assailant through to the large kitchen, where he was thrown on the floor. The guy revived after cold water had been poured over his face. Ron proceeded to explain the benefits of paying protection money. To illustrate the point, we emptied the contents of his cupboards onto the floor. Crockery and jam jars smashed. I used a tin opener to deal with stuff that wouldn't damage easily, then went through the flat methodically slashing furniture, carpets and other fittings.

Fat Ron told the cabbie he'd call on him very soon for some more money. Then we got back into the cab and drove to a dodgy garage owned by some of Ron's associates. They would cannibalise the vehicle and Ron would get a cut of the profits. After walking a couple of blocks to a mini-cab office, we arrived back at the brothel after a short ride. I made myself some coffee but Ron drank most of it when I went to have a shit. I considered giving him a row about this but thought better of it.

I decided to go and see how things were progressing with the snuff movie. Abel fell asleep as he fucked Tracy Lucas, so as Sarah Emin took her place, I threw cold water over his face to help revive him. Sarah had a

Chinese mother and an Afro-Caribbean father, so if a punter was drunk enough she sometimes succeeded in passing herself off as Naomi Campbell and was able to charge upwards of a grand for her services. Emin looked wearied, but not as bored as Alan who was getting more pussy than is good for a grown man.

At twenty, Angel Lopez wasn't quite the youngest fuck Alan was going to get. While Angel kept him stiff, the girls yelled at Alan to chew the ends of her hair. A tasty dish, Angel could hardly speak English, but I'm assured she's a raconteur in her native Spanish. Lopez was a big girl, so big that when she sat on top of a man he was rendered helpless. As Angel bounced up and down above Abel, I could hear our star gasping for breath. Lopez faked an orgasm, all the while taking great pains to ensure Alan didn't come.

Erica Jones had little going for her other than being the same age as Jesus when he died, thirty-three. She had a limp, a squint and a finger missing from her left hand. I'm told she had once been pretty, but five years of crack addiction had taken their toll and her pimp thought his merchandise so badly spoilt that severing a finger made little difference. Erica provided a living, breathing, shambling warning against the dangers of drug abuse. Jones was barely aware of what she was doing, and I had to remind her not to make Alan come.

Mary White was an alcoholic. I could see she wasn't getting the better paid type of work any longer. She'd had a drink problem for the best part of ten years and at twenty-seven she was too far gone in this degeneracy to reclaim either her looks or her pride. Like most prostitutes, she was a sex worker for the money and if she ever shook off her drink problem, she'd probably try some other type of employment. Mary didn't look like she enjoyed fucking Alan, but then she didn't enjoy anything other than getting out of her tree.

Sarah Becker had turned to prostitution in order to support her two kids. However, she was also sensuous and vain. Why, if it wasn't for her kids, she'd have given it out for free rather than putting a meter on it. Sarah loved her work, which she viewed as a pleasure. She liked to lie back and let any man prepared to place a score in the palm of her hand have his way with her. Sarah didn't notice Alan was looking extremely dishevelled. She liked the attention her work brought her and wasn't fussy where such consideration came from.

Samantha Meyer had a fine pair of lungs and enormous knockers. She got Alan to bury his face in them. Her usual trick was to get johns to give her a pearl necklace. However, in Alan's case she was under strict instructions not to let him come. So Sammy gave Alan's prick a few licks, then took his todger all the way down her throat. It wasn't that Meyer was gagging for it, she simply wanted brass to fund her booze habit. This was a hit and run operation with Abel's pork sword being regurgitated before he shot his load.

Jasmine Gates was bored of life. She took no pleasure from sucking cock but it was an easy way of earning money to pay for her crack. Jasmine liked smoking rocks, she liked it so much that she couldn't think about anything else. Her eyes were blank, her face lined, her clothes tattered, her hair lank, her hands shook, she had a stoop and she limped. Gates was twenty-four years old and from the lazy way she worked Alan's cock with her teeth and her tongue you'd have thought she hadn't slept for twenty-four hours. Perhaps she hadn't.

Lilith Rhodes was a runaway from an abusive father and inadequate mother. She boasted a fine set of teeth. It was a shame about the rest of her. Heroin often makes men thin and causes women to bloat out. Lilith had curves in all the right places and many more to boot. Fortunately, she knew what to do with her teeth and could make punters come in a minute flat. Not that this skill was of any use while we were making a snuff movie of Alan Abel being fucked to death. Sarah only licked, she didn't suck Alan's cock.

Kait Mouse got her professional name from a pimp with a passion for supermodels and cheap con tricks. A truly tasty dish, Kait could hardly speak English, but I'm assured she puts dictionaries to shame in her native Russian. The mafia organised the complicated travel arrangements that saw her arriving in London via Finland, Sweden and Denmark. Five years on, Mouse was still paying off her mafia debt. Kait liked anal sex because she got paid extra for it. Her arse was well stretched and rarely bled, even when her male partner was as unskilled a plumber as Alan Abel.

Pandora Underson came next and since she'd just been to the clap clinic for a diagnosis and had yet to undergo a cure, she used a rubber. Not that Pandora was worried about Alan catching the pox, her concern was solely for the hoes who'd follow her heavyweight act. Underson was a big girl, so big that when she sat on top of a man he was rendered helpless. As Pandora bounced up and down above Abel, I could hear our star gasping for breath. Underson faked an orgasm, all the while taking great pains to ensure Alan didn't come.

At thirty-seven, Laura Smith was a regular house-
wife. Laura was plain but made the most of herself with
make-up and a happy-go-lucky attitude towards life.
She'd started turning the occasional trick when her
husband was out of work and found it was a good way
to earn enough money to buy designer frocks. While
Smith wasn't shrewd, neither was she so stupid that she
didn't realise most of the men who fucked her were blind
drunk and it mattered little to them what she looked like.
They just wanted a hole in which to relieve themselves.

Now twenty-three, Shelly Johnson had been a
teenage bride. These days she was an irregular house-
wife. Her marriage had not been happy and two years
ago she'd begun an affair with one of her neighbours.
She'd agreed to leave her husband for this happily
married man, then called the whole thing off. Shelly's
neighbour separated from his wife and these days
rarely saw his children. Johnson was still with her
husband but she no longer fucked him. Right now, she
got her kicks turning tricks. Shelly was a model prostitute; she rarely drank and didn't have a drugs problem.

Elsie Rogers was a petite middle-aged divorcee
whose principal interest remained homemaking. She
had a busty 38-28-38 inch figure, blue eyes and lightly-
dyed blonde hair. She was friendly and became

particularly talkative when she got onto the subject of needlework, a pursuit at which she excelled. Elsie hoped to remarry when she found the right man, someone broadminded but dependable. However, she was discreet enough to hide her disapproval of infidelity from johns who happened to have wives. She did not expect to find a new husband among the men who came to her for sex.

Melanie Klein had a degree in psychology but was unable to find suitable white collar work after coming down from Oxford. She viewed prostitution as a different kind of therapy from the type she'd studied. Melanie didn't think her university training was wasted, she made use of it when dealing with johns and hoped one day to practice psychotherapy professionally. In the meantime, turning tricks was paying for her long and arduous years of training. Klein's other interests included theatre, cinema, art, ice hockey, going for walks and eating out. She was also a big fan of the Spice Girls.

Jessica Long had left school at sixteen and spent five years working in a shop. Unfortunately, she'd got the sack after being caught pilfering petty cash. After a spell on the dole, she'd taken to supplementing her income by turning tricks. Jessica liked going to see

Hollywood blockbusters at the cinema, eating fry ups, betting at the dog races and shopping in Oxford Street. Long was also a fan of Patsy Palmer, Bianca in the television show East Enders, who she often saw at the Sunday morning flower market in Columbia Road – where they both went to buy potted plants.

Karen Brown had moved in with her parents after falling victim to repeated bouts of domestic violence. She'd found the average john less abusive than her husband, but also colder and more perfunctory about the sexual act. Karen had a steady relationship with a bloke called Jim who'd been in her class at secondary school. Jim knew Karen turned tricks but since he was out of work and Brown paid for their drinks when they went out boozing, he couldn't very well complain. Karen went drinking every night of the week because living with her dad did her head in.

To tell the truth, watching a man being shagged to death, especially a bloke like Alan Abel who appeared reluctant to die, can get pretty tiresome. The girls were still being switched every five minutes but listing their names is unlikely to hold the attention of anyone who isn't a devotee of hardcore cinema. To help pass the time, some of the girls present began exchanging ridiculous sob stories they'd palmed off on the innumerable Christians who traipse the streets of the East End attempting to save fallen women. My contribution to this crack was putting an end to it.

No, we didn't want to find our way back to God, what we needed was the Goddess. In this state of agitation I found myself fidgeting with Alan Abel's clothes and briefcase. It turned out that these contained a sheaf of dummy documents, passports that all bore Alan's photo but different personal details. The names he was using included Barry R Brannon, Charles Montague Taylor and Richard Hatch. There were copies of several different birth certificates and a raft of sado-masochistic short stories. From the latter it became apparent that Abel that believed whipping women was a spiritual exercise.

I went to the kitchen and picked up a heavy frying pan. The snuff movie wasn't working out the way I'd planned it, I was beginning to doubt that Alan would ever die from sexual exhaustion. Jackie Joiner was giving Alan a blow job when I arrived back on the set. Applying considerable force, I used the frying pan to wipe the smug expression off Abel's face. He didn't cry, he didn't move, so I hit him with the blunt instrument again and again. Jackie tried to interfere but was ordered out of the way, she was ruining the shot.

I ran screaming from the brothel, rain lashing against my face. Eventually I calmed down. Stood on Wentworth Street waiting for a john. Took a youth by the hand and led him to Green Dragon Yard. I was Saint George, with the serpent in my mouth I pulled a knife from my pocket and sliced into the soft sack containing the john's balls. He screamed, so I slashed at his throat. Blood spurted from the jugular. I walked slowly down to Whitechapel Road. It had stopped raining. I wanted a storm to wash the blood from my hands and face.

The wind fell away and there was a dead calm, a sultry heat and that prevailing intensity which, on the approach of thunder, strongly affects persons of a sensitive nature. The stillness of the air grew quite oppressive, and the silence was so marked that snoring and the creaking of old stairs could be heard like a discord in the great harmony of nature's silence. A strange sound came from far away, and high overhead the air began to carry a peculiar, faint, hollow booming. Then without warning the tempest broke. With a rapidity which, at the time, seemed incredible.

I knew intuitively that I'd made the whole aspect of nature convulse. The wind roared like thunder, and blew with such force that it was with difficulty that even strong men kept their feet, or clung with grim clasp to lamp-posts. To add to the distresses and dangers of the time, masses of fog came drifting off the Thames. Grey, wet clouds, which swept by in ghostly fashion, so dank and damp and cold that it needed but little effort of imagination to think that the spirits of earlier generations were greeting the living with the touch of death.

Many a night walker shuddered as the wreaths of mist swept by. At times the mist cleared, and the streets for some distance could be seen in the glare of the lightning, which now came thick and fast, followed by such sudden peals of thunder that the whole sky overhead seemed trembling under the shock of the footsteps of the storm. Some of the scenes thus revealed were of immeasurable grandeur and of absorbing interest. There are such things as primitive instincts and these instincts rule the human heart. Some of us even have the evidence that these instincts exist.

Disregarding the evidence of our own vast and immeasurably happy experiences, the teachings and the records of the past give proof enough for sane people not to doubt the power of these urges. I admit that at first I was a sceptic. Were it not that through long years I have trained myself to keep an open mind,

I could not have believed until such time as that fact thundered on my ear – I prove! I prove! Had I known at the first what now I know – nay, had I even guessed – I would have led a very different life.

I am stronger now, and being stronger, have yet more power to work evil. The beast I have become is a Goddess as strong as twenty men. I am of a cunning more than mortal, for my cunning be the growth of ages; soon I shall have the aids of necromancy, which is, as etymology implies, divination by means of the dead, and all the dead I despatch will be reanimated and made to obey my commands. I am a brute, and more than a brute. I am a Goddess and can, within limitations, appear in any form I choose.

I can direct the elements – the storm, the fog, the thunder. I can command all the meaner things – the rat, the owl, the bat, the moth, the fox and the wolf, I can grow and become small. I can at times vanish and become unknown. I am a foul thing of the night, without heart or conscience, preying on the bodies and the souls of weak men. I go abhorred by all, a blot on the face of London. You have denounced me as a monster, made me what I am. Now I will reclaim this corruption as my own.

I met another john as I made my way up Brick Lane.

He wanted to be tied up and whipped. For fifty knicker I was more than willing to oblige. We walked to his loft apartment, a conversion on Commercial Street. There was a tiger skin rug on the floor. I told my victim I'd secure him to his home gym. He enjoyed being bound but wasn't happy when I stuffed a partially used bar of soap in his mouth and used a gag to hold it in place. But since he could no longer talk, he didn't really complain.

I explained that I was giving the full service. I expected my victim to look delighted. Getting himself ritually sex murdered for fifty quid had to be the greatest bargain of all time. I found a pair of bolt cutters and cut the little finger off the john's left hand. If he hadn't been gagged I think he would have screamed. Poor darling. Next I dropped my knickers and rubbed my pussy in his anxious face. This didn't rouse even a flicker of excitement, so I pulled back and began to finger myself while running my tongue around my lips.

I picked up the severed pinkie and stuck it into my cunt, so that it went in as far as the knuckle with the bloody end sticking out. I splayed my legs so that the john could see what I'd done. I grinned and spoke about the extreme lengths to which sexual objectification might be taken. Paraphrasing some of the papers that I'd found in Alan Abel's briefcase, I explained that

prior to the Fall all beings had been hermaphrodites –
but when the Goddess divided us into men and women,
it was the chicks who got to represent radical evil.

I bent down and scooped the john's droopy dick into
my mouth while running my fingers gently under his
corpulent balls. He didn't go stiff. I was enjoying myself
so much, it was several minutes before I picked up the
bolt cutters and severed the little finger from the john's
right hand, this time taking it off at the joint with the
knuckle rather than down near the palm. Fear gazed
back at me through terrified eyes and I felt compelled to
justify my behaviour to this stranger since I fully
intended to murder him. My explanation ran as follows.

Scientists tell us they know all that is worth
knowing about man, which statement, of course,
includes woman. They trace him from his remotest
origin. They show us how his bones changed and his
shape modified. Also how, under the influence of his
needs and passions, his intelligence developed from
something very humble. They demonstrate conclu-
sively that there is nothing in man which the
dissecting-table will not explain. That his aspirations
towards another life have their root in the fear of
death. That his affinities with the past are merely inherited from remote ancestors who lived in that past.

Rationalists say that everything noble about man is but the fruit of expediency or a veneer of civilisation, while everything base must be attributed to the instincts of his dominant and primeval nature. Man, in short, is an animal who, like every other animal, is finally subdued by his environment and takes his colour from his surroundings, as certain cattle do from the red soil of Devon. Such are the facts of science. Then perhaps something gives us pause and causes doubts, the old satanic doubts, to arise again deep in our hearts, and with them a yet diviner hope.

Perchance when all is said, so we think to ourselves, man is something more than an animal. Perchance he has known the past, the far past, and will know the future, the far, far future. Perchance the dream is true, and he does indeed possess what for convenience is called an immortal soul, that may manifest itself in one shape or another. That may sleep for ages, but, waking or sleeping, still remains itself, indestructible as the matter of the universe. Perchance what the rationalist culture denounces as the beast within, is actually a miraculous survival of the pagan spirit.

At this crucial point in my justification of the murder I was about to commit, I realised my victim had passed out. His breathing was shallow but he was still alive. I figured it didn't really make much difference whether he consciously heard me or not, since whatever I said would be forever imprinted on his id. What was happening to him wasn't personal. I was possessed by the spirit of Ma-Mee and since her tomb had been desecrated she wanted revenge. Smith had disappeared without a trace, so I'd randomly picked the unconscious john as a diabolic substitute.

I undid the gag I'd placed over Smith's mouth. By this time I'd convinced myself the substitute was Smith, and although he was actually Francis Galton, I became so confused about his identity that I will refer to him as Smith from now on. Not only was Smith a leading proponent of eugenics, he was so obsessed by statistics that he would do computations about the number of pleasing, ordinary and ugly women who passed him in the street. Smith was a conservative who believed intelligence was inherited, and that the breeding capacity of the working class should be curtailed.

As I loosened the gag, the soap I'd place in Smith's mouth slipped into his gullet. I tried desperately to retrieve it. Choking, Smith came to life like some modern-day Frankenstein's monster. If I'd not tied him down so securely, he might have lurched forward and dislodged the cake of soap from his windpipe. Instead, his face turned bright red and some rather peculiar gurgling sounds were strangled in his throat. Instead of weathering this trauma, Smith succumbed to it, and thereby missed out on the sex murder that was his birthright. I was, to put it mildly, gutted.

I raved and remonstrated with him but he was impervious to both rhetoric and reason. He was not supposed to die at this point, death was to come later. I accused him of all sorts of things, using words and phrases that sounded crude even in the mouth of a whore. Party pooper was the mildest term of reproach. My nerves were frayed and all seemed lost. I was in two minds about what to do next. Whether to proceed regardless or go out and find a fresh victim. I dropped my knickers, fingered my clit and invoked Sol's guidance.

There were trampings and a sound like something heavy being laid on the floor, such, for instance, as must have been made when the mummy of a Pharaoh was set down for its last journey to the western bank of the Nile. There was a strange play of light. This light was pale and ghostly, though very penetrating and tinged with blue. At first it arose to form a kind of fan or fountain. But what was this that stood at the door now, radiating glory? It was Osiris himself, God of the Dead, the Egyptian saviour of the world!

I found a lethargy creeping over me. I lay down, but could not quite sleep, so I got up and looked out of the window. Mist was spreading, and I could see it lying thick against the building opposite me, as though it were stealing up to the windows. I was so tired that I crept back into Smith's bed, and pulled the duvet over my head. I thought I was too tired to sleep, but I must have dropped off. My dreams were very peculiar, and typified the way that waking thoughts become merged with, or continued in, dreams.

Osiris stood in his mummy-cloths, wearing the feathered crown and holding in his hands, which projected from an opening in the wrappings, the crook and the scourge of power. He never moved, simply stood there, splendid and fearful, his calm, benign face staring into nothingness. The blue light began to grow. Long tongues of it shot forward, which joined themselves together, illuminating the room with orgone energy. All around stood the kings and queens of Egypt. As though at a given signal, they bowed to him, and ere the tinkling of their ornaments had died away, Osiris was gone.

I dreamt I was asleep, and waiting for Smith to return. I was anxious about him, and I was powerless to act. My brain was weighted, so that nothing could proceed at the usual pace. Therefore I slept uneasily and dreamt vividly. Suddenly I realised that the air was heavy, and dank, and cold. I pulled back the duvet from my face. It occurred to me that I had not shut the window before I'd got into bed. I would have got up and corrected this oversight, but some leaden lethargy seemed to chain my limbs and even my will.

In the place of Osiris stood another: Isis, the Mother of Mystery, her deep eyes looking forth from beneath the jewelled vulture-cap. The congregation bowed and she disappeared like mist in the sun. In her place stood yet another, a radiant, lovely being, who held in her hand the Sign of Life, and wore upon her head the symbol of the shining disc – Hathor, Goddess of Love. A third time the congregation bowed, and she too was gone. There was the long-necked Khu-en-aten, talking rather angrily to the imperial Rameses II. Beside them stood Ma-Mee.

I lay still and endured; that was all. I closed my eyes, but could still see through my eyelids. The mist grew thicker and thicker, and I could see now how it came in, for I could see it like smoke – or with the white energy of boiling water – pouring in, not through the window, but through the joinings of the door. It got thicker and thicker, till it seemed as if it became concentrated into a sort of pillar of cloud in the room, through the top of which I could see red light shining like a bloodshot eye.

Ma-Mee was tall and somewhat fair-complexioned with slumberous, dark eyes. On her face gleamed a mystic smile. She wore a robe of simple white and a purple-broidered apron, a crown of golden uraei with turquoise eyes was set upon her dark hair and on her breast and arms were a gold necklace and bracelets. Dense darkness fell upon the place, and with it a silence that was morbid, like a sudden depletion of life-giving orgones. At length the light came again, first as a blue spark, then in upward pouring rays, until finally it pervaded everything.

Things began to whirl through my brain just as the cloudy column was now whirling in the room. The red light held a morbid fascination for me and seemed to shine on my face through the thick fog. All became black darkness. The last conscious effort which imagination made was to show me a shining white face bending over me out of the mist. I must be careful of such dreams, for they could unseat my fragile reason. In dreams begin responsibilities. These dreams tired me more than if I had not slept at all. I struggled up and on.

A young man dressed in the robes and insignia of an

early dynasty came forward and stood between Pharaoh Menes and those who reigned after him. Nearby stood a man of middle age, with a thoughtful brow, who held in his hand a wand and wore the feathers and insignia of the heir to the throne of Egypt and of a high priest of Amen. He was Khaemuas, son of Rameses the Great, the mightiest magician that ever was in Egypt, who of his own will withdrew himself from Earth before the time came to sit upon the mortal throne.

The general feeling, as it came over me, was like that which takes possession of the mind in dreams – when one feels oneself sleeping alone, utterly divided from all call or hearing of friends, doors open that should be shut, or unlocked that should be triply secured, the very walls gone, barriers swallowed up by unknown abysses, nothing around one but a world of illimitable night, whisperings at a distance, correspondence going on between darkness and darkness, like one deep calling to another, and the dreamer's own heart the centre from which the whole network of this unimaginable chaos radiates.

The blank privations of silence and darkness became powers the most positive and awful. A blind misery of fear fell upon me, so much the worse than any anguish of a beleaguered fighter awaiting the final blows of an unleashed fury raining unstemmed from a victorious enemy. By how much the shadowy, the uncertain, the infinite, is at all times more potent in mastering the mind than a danger that is known, measurable, palpable and human. My very bones and ligaments were seized with terror. I quaked and was consumed by the intense frenzy of this violent and uncontrollable trembling.

Agencies of fear, as of any other passion, and, above all, of any passion felt in communion with thousands, in which the heart beats in conscious sympathy with an entire city, through all its regions, high and low, young and old, strong and weak. Such agencies avail to raise and transfigure the natures of mortals. Mean minds become elevated. Dull men become eloquent. And when matters come to such a crisis, the public feeling, as made known by voice, gesture, manner or words, is such that no stranger could represent it to his fancy. I imagined the dead might speak.

I struggled over to where Smith lay strapped to his exercise machine. He was still stone cold dead, so I cut off his dick and flushed it down the lavatory. Then I took a jar of honey from the kitchen and fashioned him a new prick from the sticky substance. Next, using a needle and thread, I stitched Smith's two severed fingers back onto his delightfully mutilated hands. At last, Smith was perfect in every way and I rather liked the fact he was dead. Immensely satisfied, I decided to tell him some home truths about the commodification of sex.

Smith was silent. I turned the words he'd exchanged with me over in my mind. He'd not said much before he'd died. As I left Smith's apartment, a crowd surged into the street. A man in rags addressed them with a degree of frankness that left little to be desired. I slunk away unnoticed. A more miserable night for an out-of-doors excursion I could hardly have chosen. The rain was like a mist, and was not only drenching me to the skin, but it was rendering it difficult to see more than a short distance in any direction.

The neighbourhood was badly lit. I had taken the first turning to the left, and, at the moment, had been glad to take it. In the darkness, the locality which I was entering appeared unfinished. I seemed to be leaving civilisation behind me. The path was unpaved, the road rough and uneven as if it had never been properly made. Exactly where I was I could not tell. I had a faint notion that, if I only kept on long enough, I should strike some part of Shadwell. How long I would have to keep on I could only guess.

Like a wanton wretch, I lurched forward and fell upon my knees. Such was my backboneless state that for some seconds I remained where I was, half disposed to let things slide, accept the good fate had sent me and make a night of it just there. A long night it would have been, I fancy, stretching from time unto eternity. Having regained my feet, I had gone perhaps another couple of hundred yards along the road when there came over me again that overpowering giddiness which, I take it, was born of my agony of alcoholism and drug abuse.

I staggered and stumbled helplessly against a low wall which, just there, was at the side of the path. Without it I should have fallen in a crumpled heap. The attack appeared to last for hours, I suppose it was only seconds. And when I came to myself, it was as though I had been aroused from a swoon of sleep – woken, to an extremity of shrieking pain. I looked about me in a kind of impotent frenzy. As I did so, I became conscious that behind me was a house. It was not particularly large, nor was it small.

A bow window was open. The bottom centre sash was raised about six inches. I mentally photographed all the little details of the house in front of which I was standing with what amounted to a drug-induced preternatural perception. Visions. Surging seas. Shooting stars. An instant before, the world swam before my eyes. I saw nothing. Now I saw everything with a clearness that was utterly shocking. Above all, I saw the open window. I stared at it, conscious as I did so of a curious catching of my breath. It was so near to me, so very near.

I alone was at the mercy of the sodden night. There was no one to see what I might do, no one to care. I needed to fear no spy. Perhaps the house was empty. Nay, probably. It was my plain duty to knock at the door, rouse the inmates and call attention to their oversight, the open window. The least they could do would be to reward me for my pains. But suppose the place was empty, what would be the use of knocking? It would be to make a useless clatter. Possibly to disturb the neighbourhood for nothing.

And, even if the people were at home, I might go unrewarded. I had learned in life's hard school the world's boundless ingratitude. To have caused the window to be closed – and then to be no better for it after all, out in the cold and the rain – better anything than that. In such a situation, too late, I should say to myself, that mine had been the conduct of a fool. And I should say it justly too, to be sure. Leaning over the low wall I found that I could very easily put my hand inside the room.

How still it was! Beyond doubt, the place was empty. I decided to push the window up another inch, so as to enable me to reconnoitre. If anyone caught me in the act, then there would be an opportunity to describe the circumstances, and to explain how I was just on the point of giving the alarm. Only, I must go carefully. In such damp weather it was probable that the sash would creak. Not a bit of it. It moved readily and noiselessly. This silence of the sash so emboldened me that I raised it more than I intended.

Lifting myself by means of the sill I slipped my legs into the room. The moment I did so I became conscious that, at any rate, it wasn't entirely unfurnished. The floor was carpeted. I have had my feet on some good carpets in my time. I know what good carpets are, but never have I stood upon a softer one than that. It reminded me, somehow, even then, of the turf in Richmond Park. It caressed my instep, and sprang up beneath my weary tread. To my poor, travel-worn feet, it was ostentatious luxury after the potholed road.

When I had taken four such steps without encountering an obstacle, I began to wish that I hadn't seen the house. That I had passed it by. That I had not gone through the window. That I were safely out of it again. I became aware that there was something with me in the room. There was nothing ostensible to lead me to such a conviction. It may be that my faculties were unnaturally keen, but I knew there was something lurking in the dark. What was more, I had a horrible persuasion that my every movement was being watched.

Whatever was in the room, in the dark room, must surely be as great a coward as me to permit, unchecked, my burglarious entry. Since I had been allowed to enter, the probability was that I should be at liberty to retreat, and I was sensible of a much keener desire to retreat than I had ever had to enter. I had to put the greatest amount of pressure upon myself before I could summon up sufficient courage to enable me even to turn my head upon my shoulders, and the moment I did so I turned it back again.

The light which snapped on was unexpected. It stopped me in my tracks. I was just recovering when a voice told me to keep still. There was a quality to the tone which I cannot describe. Not only an accent of command, but something saturnine. It was a little guttural, a man's voice, and I had no doubt that it belonged to a pimp. It was the most disagreeable speech I had ever heard, and it had on me the most obnoxious effect. For it was as though there was nothing else for me to do but to obey it.

I turned round mechanically, like an automaton. Such passivity was worse than undignified, it was galling in a whore, I knew that well. I resented it with secret rage. But in that room, in that presence, I was invertebrate. When I turned I found myself confronting someone who was lying in bed. At the head of the bed was a shelf. On the shelf was a small lamp which gave the most brilliant light I had ever seen. It caught me full in the eyes, having on me such a blinding effect that, for some seconds, I could see nothing.

Throughout the whole of the strange interview which followed, I cannot affirm that I saw anything clearly. The dazzling glare caused dancing specks to obscure my hazy vision. Yet after an interval of time, I did see something and what I saw I would have rather left sight unseen. I perceived someone in front of me lying in a bed. At first I had my doubts about it being human. But, afterwards, I knew it was a pimp – for this reason, if for no other – he told me that as long as I was his whore, he would protect me.

It was the pimp who finally broke the silence. I was speechless. Finally I spoke to answer him. There was this odd thing about the words I uttered, that they came from me, not in response to my will power, but in response to his. It was not I who willed that I should speak, it was he. What he willed I should say, I said. Just that, and nothing more. For the time being I was no longer a free individual, my personality was merged in his. I was, in the extremest sense, an example of pure passive obedience.

He instructed me to undress. I obeyed, letting my sodden, shabby clothes fall anyhow upon the floor. A look came over his face as I stood naked in front of him, which, if it was meant to be a smile, was a satyr's smile, and filled me with a sensation of shuddering repulsion. He devoured me with his glances and rubbed my clitoris with his finger. He went to a cupboard which was in a corner of the room. It was full of garments which might have formed the stock-in-trade of a costumier whose customers were sexual fetishists.

A long dark cloak hung on a peg. His hand moved towards it, apparently of its own volition. I put it on, its ample folds falling to my feet. I looked him in the face, and was immediately aware of something going from me – the capacity, as it were, to be myself. His eyes grew larger, till I became lost in their immensity. He moved his hand, doing something to me, I know not what, cutting the solid ground from underneath my feet, so that I fell headlong to the ground. Where I fell, there I lay, utterly beyond redemption.

What had happened to me I could not guess. That I probably wore some of the external evidences of death my instinct told me. I felt as a woman might feel who had actually died – as, in moments of speculation, in years gone by, I had imagined it as quite possible she would feel. It is very far from certain that consciousness necessarily expires alongside our mortal shell. I continually asked myself if I was dead – the inquiry pressed itself on me with awful iteration. Does the body die, and the conscious self – the I, the ego – still live on?

The hours passed. By slow degrees, the silence was eclipsed. Sounds of traffic, of hurrying footsteps, life, were ushers of the morning. Outside the window sparrows twittered, a cat mewed, a dog barked, there was the clatter of a milk van. Shafts of light stole past the blind, increasing in intensity. It still rained, now and again it pattered against the pane. The wind must have shifted, because, for the first time, there came, on a sudden, the clang of a distant clock striking the hour – eight. Then, with the interval of a lifetime between each chiming, nine – ten – eleven.

A face looked into mine, and, in front of me were his dreadful eyes. And then, whether I was dead or living, I told myself that this could be nothing human. Nothing fashioned in Loki's image could wear such a shape as this creature. Fingers were pressed into my cheeks, they were thrust into my mouth, they touched my staring eyes, shut my eyelids, then opened them again, and – horror of horrors – a tongue was pushed into my mouth – the soul of something evil entered into me in the guise of a kiss. Then the occult pimp slowly stood up.

He moved away from me. I heard a door open and shut, and knew that he was gone. He was gone all day and for all I knew, gone for good. I had no knowledge of his issuing out into the street, but he must have done so, because the house appeared deserted. On numerous occasions through that long and torpid afternoon, people outside endeavoured to attract the attention of whoever was within. Vehicles drew up in front, their stopping being followed by more or less assiduous assaults upon a door bell. But in every case their appeals remained unheeded.

A prostitute who worked for my domineering pimp arrived at the house, and let herself in. She was of above average height, slender, and wonderfully graceful. Although her movements were languid, there was absolutely nothing in her appearance to indicate an invalid. Her complexion was rich and brilliant. Her features were small and beautifully formed. Her eyes large, dark, and lustrous. Her hair was quite wonderful, I never saw hair so magnificently thick and long when it was down about her shoulders. It was exquisitely fine and soft, and in colour a very rich dark brown, with something of gold.

Tania Gibbs explained that increasingly heavy policing made the traditional haunts of our trade unviable. The girls had moved east to Tower Hamlets Cemetery where, dressed in widow's weeds, they were able to solicit business unmolested by the cops. I was to accompany Tania to the graveyard. We would turn tricks. But first I was to be instructed in an even more important task. The john I'd used as a diabolical substitute for Smith had been a fully human incarnation of Osiris. Since I'd inadvertently murdered the solar god, I was to be initiated into the mysteries of resurrecting him.

I was given the signs and the keys, the chants and spells, the divers magical instructions. Once I'd mastered the theory and practice of Egyptian necromancy, Tania and I dressed in black lace and made our way to

Tower Hamlets Cemetery. It was dark. The body of Osiris was laid out on a tomb. Tania bent over him; her sweet lips touched his brow. The perfume from her breath and hair beat upon him. The light of her wondrous eyes searched out his very soul, reading the answer that was written there. This god was dead but would soon live.

Eventually a hand stretched out, but the demoniacal corpse which I had so generously reanimated keeled over and died at the very moment of his resurrection. No mere mortal could support the horror of that countenance. A mummy again endued with life could not be so hideous as solar wretch Osiris. I nearly sank to the ground through feelings of languor and extreme weakness. Mingled with this horror, I felt the bitterness of disappointment. Dreams that had been my food and pleasant rest were now become a hell to me – and the change was so rapid, the overthrow so complete!

Abandoning the resurrection of Osiris as a farce – perhaps I'd mispronounced some rudimentary phrase in my incantations – I looked for gainful employment elsewhere. Along the grass track I saw, under the moon, a strange procession. It moved on, quickly but noiselessly. A sable litter, borne by four men, a fake funeral cortege, in reality johns on the lookout for pussy. As the litter halted, from the long, dark shadow which it cast upon the turf, the figure of a woman emerged and stood before me. The outlines of her shape were lost in the loose folds of a black mantle.

The features of her face were hidden by a black veil, except for dark solemn eyes. Her stature was lofty, her bearing majestic. One of the men drew her away from the group into a neighbouring copse of non-flowering conifers – mystic trees, never changing the hues of their dark-green leaves, ever shifting the tints of their black-grey, shedding bark. For some moments I gazed on two nearly human forms, dimly seen by the glinting moonlight through the gaps in the foliage. She was on her knees and he moaned. A blow job is a matter of trust.

Turning my eyes, I saw, standing close at my side, a man whom I had not noticed before. His footstep, as it stole towards me, had fallen on the sward without sound. His dress was one of mourning, and differed little from that of his companions, both in shape and colour – a dark suit, white shirt and black tie. His features were those of a bird of prey. The beak of the eagle, but the eye of the vulture. His cheeks were hollow. His arms, crossed on his breast. His flies were undone and his erect cock protruded from them.

In the john's skeleton form there was a something

that conveyed the idea of a serpent's suppleness and strength. As his hungry, watchful eyes met my own startled gaze, I recoiled impulsively with that inward warning of danger. At my movement the man inclined his head in a submissive salutation and flashed a score that he held in his right palm. I took the money and lifting my skirt, spread myself against a rectilinear gravestone. The skeletal man advanced and I rolled a condom down his rigid member. Moments later, he was inside me, spilling his seed within the sheath.

One of the johns entered the litter, and the veiled whore drew the black curtains round him. The strumpet turned to me, and her veil was withdrawn. The face on which I gazed was severe but wondrously beautiful. There was neither youth nor age, but beauty, mature and majestic as that of a marble Demeter. The woman let fall her veil and after moving a few feet in my directions, stopped short of me. There, as she stood, the moon shone full on her wasted form, on her face, resolute, cheerful, and proud, despite its hollowed outlines and sicklied hues.

The harlot turned and made her way back to the litter. Signalling silently, she slipped an arm around a john. Together they took a coffer and fuel from her conveyance. The logs were placed where the moonlight fell fullest on the cemetery – a part of it already piled for a fire, the rest of it heaped confusedly close at hand. By the pile she laid down the coffer. And there she stood, her arms folded under her mantle, her dark image seeming darker still as the moonlight whitened all the ground from which she rose, in most graceful slow motion.

I watched in silence as she calmly made her weird preparations. On the ground a wide circle was traced by a small rod, on its tip a sponge saturated with combustible fluid, so that a pale, lambent flame followed the course of the rod as the whore wielded it, burning the herbage over which it played, and leaving a distinct ring. On this circle were placed twelve small lamps, fed with fluid from the same vessel and lit by the same rod. The light emitted by these lamps was even more effulgent than that which so vividly circled the ring.

Within the circumference the hooker traced certain geometrical figures in which I recognised the interlaced triangles which my own hand, in the spell enforced on a sleepwalker, had described on the floor of the pimp's residence the previous night. The figures were traced like the circle, in flame, and at the point of each triangle – four in number – was placed a lamp, brilliant as those on the ring. This task performed, the cauldron, resting on an iron tripod, was placed over the woodpile. And then a john, previously inactive and unheeding, slowly advanced, kneeling by the pile to light it.

The dry wood crackled and the flame burst forth, licking the rims of the cauldron with tongues of fire. I flung into the cauldron various particles I had collected, poured over them first a liquid, colourless as water, from the largest of the vessels drawn from a coffer, and then, more sparingly, drops from small crystal phials. Having surmounted their first impulse of awe, the johns watched these proceedings, curious yet disdainful, as those who watch the mummeries of an enchanter on the stage. However, they were more than willing to part with ready cash when I offered them sex.

One hour passed away. The faggots under the cauldron burned clear in the sullen, sultry air. The materials within began to seethe, and their colour, at first dull and turbid, changed to a pale-rose hue. From time to time the veiled woman replenished the fire. After she had done so – and when she wasn't servicing a john – she seated herself close by the pyre with her head bowed and her face hidden under her veil. The lights in the lamps and along the ring and the triangles now began to pale. I resupplied their nutriment from a crystal vessel.

Nothing strange startled my eye or my ear beyond the rim of the circle – nothing audible, save, at a distance, the musical wheel-like click of couples rutting, and, farther still, in the sleeping city, the howl of dogs that never barked. Nothing visible but tower blocks and overpasses silvered by the moon, girding the eastern flank of the square mile. I passed the time giving oral, anal and quick hand jobs (for down-at-heel johns with little money to spend). The reversibility of sex and death is never more apparent than when whores turn tricks in a graveyard.

The second hour passed like the first. I had taken my stand close by the cauldron with a john, when I felt the ground vibrate beneath my feet and, looking up, it seemed as if all the buildings beyond the graveyard were heaving like the swell of the sea, as if, in the air itself, there was a perceptible tremor. Neither the ring nor the lamps had again required replenishing. Perhaps their light was being exhausted less quickly, as gathering clouds meant they were no longer exposed to the rays of the moon. Outside the circle, the stillness was profound.

And about this time I saw distinctly in the distance a vast eye. It drew nearer and nearer, seeming to move from the ground at the height of some lofty giant. Its gaze riveted me. My blood curdled in the blaze from its angry ball, and now as it advanced larger and larger, other eyes grew out from the space in its rear – numbers on numbers, like the spearheads of some army, seen afar by pale warders of battlements doomed to the dust. My voice long refused an utterance to my awe. At length it burst forth, shrill and loud.

My accomplice rose at this abjuration. Her veil was withdrawn, and the blaze of the fire flushed, as with the rosy bloom of youth, the grand beauty of her softened face. It was seen, detached, as it were, from her dark-mantled form. Seen through the mist of the vapours which rose from the cauldron, framing it round like the clouds that are yieldingly pierced by the light of the evening star. A moment or so later she came round from the opposite side of the fire, and bending over a john's upturned brow, kissed it solemnly. The trick fainted.

The unveiled whore's countenance grew fierce, her crest rose erect. She stretched forth her arm from her black mantle, athwart the pale front that now again bent over the cauldron – stretched it toward the haunted and hollow-sounding space beyond, in the gesture of one whose right hand has the sway of the sceptre. And then her voice stole on the air in the music of a chant, not loud yet far-reaching. So thrilling, so sweet and yet so solemn that I could at once comprehend how old legend united the spell of enchantment with the power of song.

I cannot adequately describe the effect the unveiled harlot's strange chant produced on my ear. It might be likened to the depth and the art and the soul of the singer, whose voice seemed endowed with a charm to enthral all the tribes of creation, though the language it used for that charm might to them be unknown. As the song ceased, I heard from behind sounds like those I had heard in the spaces before me – the tramp of invisible feet, the whir of invisible wings, as if armies were marching to aid against armies in march to destroy.

The sky was tinged with sulphurous hues. I replenished the lamps and the ring in front, but when I came to the sixth lamp, not a drop in the vessel that fed them was left. In a vague dismay, I looked round the half of the wide circle in rear of two prostrate figures intent on complete sexual gratification. All along that disk the light was already broken, here and there flickering up, here and there dying down. The six lamps in that half of the circle still twinkled, but faintly, as stars shrinking fast from the dawn of day.

The liquid which glowed in the cauldron had taken

on a splendour that mocked all comparisons with the lustre of gems. In its prevalent colour it had the dazzle and flash of rubies. Out from the mass of the molten red broke coruscations of all prismal hues. No longer was there scum upon the surface, only a rosy vapour floating up, and quickly lost in the sulphurous air. And these coruscations formed, on the surface of the molten ruby, literally the shape of a rose, its leaves made distinct in their outlines by sparks of emerald and diamond and sapphire.

Tania Gibbs found me. We exchanged a few words, a very few words, then drank from the cauldron. It was time to knock off. Tania gave me the pimp's cut of her earnings, alongside the percentage owed by other whores. I took the money, adding it to my own. Then an invisible force drew me back the way I'd come, carrying a bottle of the elixir from the cauldron to my inhuman master. I didn't know where I was going, I didn't need to know, some sinister force guided me alone and on foot through the streets of east London.

I pulled up sharply, as if a brake had been suddenly and even mercilessly applied to bring me to a standstill. In front of the window I stood shivering. A shower had commenced, the falling rain was blown before the breeze. I was in a terrible sweat, yet tremulous as with cold. Covered with mud, bruised, cut, and bleeding. As piteous an object as you would care to see. Every limb in my body was aching; every muscle was exhausted. Both mentally and physically I'd gone beyond my limit, but I was held up by a spell put upon me,

I awoke much later and after what seemed like hours, heard the lock turned and the front door open with a furious bang. It was closed as loudly as it was opened. Then the door of the room in which I lay was dashed open, with the same display of clamour. Footsteps came hurrying in, the door was slammed with a force which shook the house to its foundations. There was a rustling of bed-clothes, the brilliant illumination of two nights before, and a clipped voice, which I had good reason to remember, told me to stand to attention.

I stood up, automatically, at the word of command, facing towards the bed. There, between the sheets, with his head resting on his hand in the attitude in which I had last seen him, was the pimp – the same, yet not the same. That the man in the bed was the one whom, to my cost, I had suffered myself to stumble on two nights before, there could, of course, not be the faintest doubt. And yet, directly I saw him, I recognised that some astonishing alteration had taken place in his appearance. To begin with, he seemed much younger.

He made a movement with his hand, and at once it happened, as on a previous evening, that a metamorphosis took place in the very abysses of my being. I woke from my torpor. I came out of death and was alive again. However, I was far from being mistress of my own destiny. I realised that this evil pimp exerted a mesmeric force over me which I had never dreamt one creature could exercise over another. At least I was no longer in any doubt as to whether I was or was not dead. I knew I was alive.

I was instructed to dress myself in Victorian widow's weeds. A most ridiculous outfit of several black petticoats beneath a black dress, black lace everywhere and the most distasteful black bonnet. I went to the window. Drawing up the blind and unlatching the sash, I threw it open and, clad as I was, I clambered through it into the open air. I was not only incapable of resistance, I was incapable of distinctly formulating the desire to offer resistance. Some compelling influence moved me hither and thither, with complete disregard for whether I had any desire to obey these commands.

When I found myself in the open air, I felt a sense of exultation at having escaped from the miasmic atmosphere of that room of unholy memories. And a faint hope began to dawn within me that, as I increased the distance between myself and that eldrich chamber, I might shake off something of the nightmare helplessness which numbed and tortured me. I lingered for a moment by the window, then stepped over the short dividing wall into the street. Then again I tarried. My condition was one of dual personality – while physically I was bound, mentally I was free.

I realised what a ridiculous figure I must be cutting, parading about at night in frilly black weeds. I do believe that if my oppressor had only permitted me to attire myself in a short skirt and tight top, I would have turned tricks with a light heart. I believe, too, that my consciousness of the incongruity of my attire increased my sense of helplessness, and that, had I been dressed as whores are wont to be, who take their walks abroad, he would not have found in me, on that occasion, the facile instrument which in fact he did.

There was a moment when I think it possible that, if I'd gritted my teeth and strained my every nerve, I'd have shaken myself free from the bonds which shackled me. But I was so depressed by my ridiculous appearance that the moment passed before I could take advantage of it. On my way to the cemetery, I saw not a soul. There are streets in London, long lines of streets, which at a certain time of night, in a certain sort of weather, are clean deserted. In which there is neither foot-passenger nor vehicle – not even a john.

I stopped opposite the graveyard. As I stood wondering what would happen next, some strange impulse mastered me and immediately I found myself scrambling up the outside wall as I attempted to make my way into the cemetery. Neither by nature nor by education am I a gymnast. I doubt whether, previously, I had ever attempted to climb anything more difficult than a step ladder. The result was that, though the impulse might be given me, the skill could not, and I had only ascended a yard or so when, losing my footing, I came slithering down upon my back.

In a moment I was on my feet again and impelled to climb, only to come to grief once more. This time the demon, or whatever it was that had entered into me, appreciating the impossibility of getting me to the top of the wall, directed me to skirt about it. In what direction I was going I did not know. I was like a sleeper flying through the phantasmagoric happenings of a dream, knowing neither how nor whither. Every detail of my involuntary actions was projected upon my brain in a series of pictures with bright and vivid outlines.

There were johns, plenty of johns and I made good

money for my pimp. He was pleased. The johns pretty much resembled one another. One was a taxi driver, the next a cop. The taxi driver was a former cop. I had a despatch rider, a van driver, a long distance lorry driver, a cycle courier. Mostly the johns who frequented Tower Hamlets Cemetery lived in London, but they had grown up all over the place. For example – Jetty Road, Alresford. Sweethope Avenue, Ashington. New Road, Banbury. Regency Close, Bishop's Stortford. Creswicke Road, Bristol. Church View, Broxbourne. Langley Terrace, Jarrow.

I got a sexton who was digging up a grave to remove the earth from a coffin-lid, and I opened it. By confronting death I gave some ease to myself. I fantasised that I was sleeping the last sleep by that sleeper, with my heart stopped and my cheek frozen against the corpse. And had the cadaver been dissolved into earth, or worse, what would I have fantasised about then? Of dissolving with this body and being happier still! Should I have dreaded any change of that sort? Not me, I expected such a transformation on raising the lid.

I was pleased that death should not have commenced until I had shared it with this stiff. Besides, unless I'd received a distinct impression of those passionless features, my strange longing wouldn't have been satiated. It began oddly. I strongly believe in ghosts. I'm convinced that they can and do exist among us. There came a fall of snow. It blew bleak as winter – all round was solitary. Being alone and conscious that two yards of loose earth was the sole barrier between me and hundreds of cadavers, I thought to myself, I'll have them all in my arms yet.

If they be cold I'll think it is the north wind chilling me, and if they be motionless, it is sleep. I got a spade from a hut and began to delve with all my might – it scraped a coffin. I fell to work with my hands. The wood commenced cracking about the screws. I was on the point of attaining my object, when it seemed I heard a sigh from someone above, bending down close to the edge of the grave. If I can only get this off, I thought, I wish they would shovel earth over us both.

I wrenched at it still more desperately. There was another sigh, close at my ear. I appeared to feel the warm breath of it displacing the sleet-laden wind. I knew no living thing in fllesh and blood was by, but as surely as you perceive the approach of some substantial body in the dark though it cannot be seen, so certainly I felt that a horny john was there: not under me, but on the earth. A sudden sense of relief flowed from my heart through every limb. I relinquished my labour of agony and turned consoled, unspeakably consoled.

A presence was with me, it remained while I refilled the grave. I was sure a mute john accompanied me, and I could not help talking to him. I felt him by me, I could almost see him, and yet could not. I ought to have sweated blood then, from the anguish of my yearning, from the fervour of my supplications to have but one glimpse. I had not one. He showed himself an infernal devil to me. Keeping my nerves at such a stretch that, if they had not resembled catgut, they would long ago have relaxed to feebleness.

As I walked up and down the gravelled pathways, the cemetery took on new shapes and angles. A church sprouted before me. The churchyard, to hide the tombstones from which the parapet had been erected, spontaneously filled with quaint old monuments, including broken-nosed cherubs, some of them dating from a comparatively early period. The porch, its sculptured niches deprived of their saints by puritan hands, was still rich and beautiful in all its carved detail. On the seat inside, an old whore was sitting. She did not rise but mumbled and muttered inarticulately to herself in a sulky undertone.

I was aware though nonetheless that, the moment I

approached her, a light gleamed suddenly in the old crone's eyes, and that her glance was fixed upon me. A faint thrill of recognition seemed to pass like a flash through her palsied body. I knew not why, but I was dimly afraid of the old harlot. She tottered off and took a seat on the edge of a depressed vault down in the churchyard close by, eyeing me still with a weird and curious glance, something like the look of a parched traveller who spies an oasis in the desert.

The old whore bent her head, and seemed to be whispering something at the door of the vault. A gaggle of harlots approached me. Among them were two hookers I'd noticed the night before. They were not only beautiful in face and figure, but on closer view I found them from the first extremely sympathetic. They at once burst into frank talk with me, with charming ease and grace of manner. They were ladies in the grain, in instinct and breeding. The taller of the two, whom the other addressed as Yolande, seemed particularly pleasing. The very name charmed me.

The other whore was named Hedda. They both possessed a certain nameless attraction that constitutes in itself the best possible introduction. I liked my new friends – their voices were so gentle, soft, and sympathetic, while for face and figure they might have sat as models to Burne-Jones or Botticelli. Their dresses, too, took my delicate fancy. They were so dainty, yet so simple. The soft black silk fell in natural folds and dimples. The only ornaments they wore were two curious brooches of very antique workmanship somewhat Celtic in design, and enamelled in blood-red on a gold background.

Each carried a flower laid loosely in her bosom. Yolande's was an orchid with long, floating streamers, in colour and shape recalling some southern lizard – dark purple spots dappled its lip and petals. Hedda's was a flower of a sort I had never before seen – the stem spotted like a viper's skin, green flecked with russet-brown, and uncanny to look upon. On either side, great twisted spirals of red-and-blue blossoms, each curled after the fashion of a scorpion's tail, strange and lurid. From the outset, something weird and witch-like about these flowers and dresses attracted me.

These costumes affected me with the half-repellent fascination of a snake for a bird. I felt such blossoms were fit for incantations and sorceries. But a lily-of-the-valley in Yolande's dark hair gave a sense of purity which assorted better with the girl's exquisite beauty. It was a moonlit evening. The breeze hardly stirred the bare boughs of the silver birches. A sprinkling of soft snow whitened the ground. The moon lit it up, falling full upon the tombs. The church and tower stood silhouetted in darkness against a cloudless expanse of starry sky in the background.

We paced once or twice up and down the gravelled walks. Strange to say, though a sprinkling of dry snow powdered the ground underfoot, the air itself was soft and balmy. Stranger still, I noticed – indeed, almost without noticing it – that though we walked three abreast, only one pair of footprints – my own – lay impressed on the snow in a long trail when we turned and retraced our steps. Yolande and Hedda must have stepped lightly indeed. Or perhaps my own feet might have been warmer or thinner shod, so as to melt the light layer of snow more readily.

The girls slipped their arms through mine. After three or four turns up and down the gravel, Yolande led the way quietly down the broad path in the direction of the church. In that bright, broad moonlight I went with them undeterred. The presence of the other girls, both wholly free from any signs of fear, took away all sense of terror or loneliness. As we strolled, I had my eyes fixed on a white tower, which merged in the silhouette against the starry sky into much the same grey and indefinite hue as the other parts of the church.

Before I quite knew where I was, I found myself at the head of the worn stone steps which led into the vault, by whose doors I had seen the wizened old crone sitting. In the pallid moonlight, with the aid of the greenish reflection from the snow, I could just read the words inscribed in Latin over the crypt's portal – *Mors janua vitae*. Yolande moved down one step. I drew back for the first time with a faint access of alarm. I freed my arms by a sudden movement and broke from my mysterious friends with a tremulous shudder.

I was far less terrified than I might have imagined beforehand would be so under such unexpected conditions. The two whores were so simple, so natural, so strangely like myself, that I could not say I was afraid of them. I shrank, it is true, from the nature of the door at which they stood, but when they told me this was where they lived – it was handy for their work, and meant that money which would otherwise be wasted on rent could service their drug habits – I received the announcement with scarcely more than a slight tremor of astonishment.

I hardly liked to say no. They seemed so anxious to show me their home. With trembling feet I moved down the first step, and then the second. Yolande kept ever one pace in front of me. As I reached the third step, the two harlots, as if moved by one design, took my wrists in their hands, not unkindly, but coaxingly. We reached the doors of the vault itself – two heavy bronze valves, meeting in the centre. Each bore a ring for a handle, pierced through a Gorgon's head embossed upon the surface. Yolande pushed them with her hand.

The doors yielded instantly to this light touch. Yolande, still in front, passed from the glow of the moon to the gloom of the vault, into which a ray of moonlight descended obliquely. For a second, a weird sight met my eyes. Yolande's face and hands and dress became self-luminous – but through them, as they glowed, I could descry every bone and joint, dimly shadowed in the dark through the luminous haze that marked her body. I drew back. What I felt could not really be described as fear, it was rather a vague sense of the profoundly mystical.

Hedda held my hand tight, and almost seemed to force me. Her hand on my wrist was strong but persuasive. It drew me without exercising the faintest compulsion. I gazed into her eyes. They were deep and tender. A strange resolution seemed to nerve her for the effort. Hedda on one side, Yolande on the other, now went before me, holding my wrists in their grasp, but rather enticing than drawing me. As each reached the gloom, the same luminous appearance I'd noticed before was discernible, and the same weird skeleton shape showed faintly through our limbs in darker shadow.

I crossed the threshold with a convulsive gasp. As I crossed it I looked down at my own dress and body. They were semi-transparent, though not quite so luminous as Yolande and Hedda. The framework of my limbs appeared within in less certain outline, yet quite dark and distinguishable. The doors swung to behind me. The three of us stood alone in the vault. Alone, for a minute or two, and then, as my eyes grew accustomed to the grey dusk of the interior, I began to perceive that the vault opened out into a large and beautiful hall.

The way was dimly lit at first, but becoming each moment more vaguely clear and more dreamily definite. Gradually I could make out great rock-hewn pillars, Romanesque in their outline or dimly Oriental, like the sculptured columns in the caves of Ellora, supporting a roof of vague and uncertain dimensions, more or less strangely dome-shaped. The effect on the whole was like that of the second impression produced by some dim cathedral, after the eyes have grown accustomed to the mellow light from the stained-glass windows, and have recovered from the blinding glare of the outer sunlight.

I turned to my companions. Yolande and Hedda stood still by my side. Their bodies were now self-luminous to a greater degree even than at the threshold, but the terrible transparency had disappeared altogether. They were once more but beautiful though strangely transfigured and more than mortal whores. Then I understood the meaning of those mystic words written over the portal – *Mors janua vitae*: Death is the gate of life – and also the interpretation of that awful vision of death dwelling within us as we crossed the threshold, for through that gate we had passed to this, the underworld.

My two guides still held my hands, one on either side. But they seemed rather to lead me on now, seductively and resistlessly, than to draw or compel me. As I moved in through the hall, with its endless vistas of shadowy pillars, seen now behind, now in dim perspective, I was gradually aware that many other people crowded its aisles and corridors. Slowly they took shape as forms more or less clad, mysterious, varied, and of many ages. Some of them wore flowing robes, at least half medieval in shape, like the two whores who had taken me there.

Some were girt merely with a light Coan sash; while others stood dimly nude in the darker recesses of the temple. All leaned eagerly forward with one mind as I approached, and regarded me with deep and sympathetic interest. A few of them murmured words – mere cabalistic sounds which at first I could not understand, but as I moved further into the hall, and saw at each step more clearly into the gloom, they began to have a meaning for me. Before long, I was aware that I understood the mute tumult of voices at once by some internal instinct.

The Shades addressed me, and I answered them. I knew by intuition that they spoke the language of the dead, and by osmosis I mastered it effortlessly. A soft and flowing tongue, this speech of the Netherworld – all vowels it seemed, without distinguishable consonants, yet dimly recalling every other tongue, and compounded, as it were, of what was common to all of them. It flowed from those shadowy lips as clouds issue inchoate from a mountain valley. It was formless, uncertain, vague, yet beautiful. I hardly knew, indeed, as it fell upon my senses, if it were sound or perfume.

Through this tenuous world of mists and shadows I moved as if in a dream, my two companions still supporting and guiding me. When we reached an inner shrine or chantry of the temple, I was dimly conscious of forms more terrible than any of those that had yet appeared to me pervading this vast, almost immeasurable cavern. It was a more austere and antique apartment than the rest. A shadowy cloister, prehistoric in its severity. It recalled to my mind something indefinitely intermediate between the huge unwrought trilithons of Stonehenge and the massive granite pillars of Philae and Luxor.

At the further end of the sanctuary a Sphinx looked down on me. At its base, on a rude megalithic throne, in solitary state, a High Priest was seated. He bore in his hand a wand. All around, a strange court of half-unseen acolytes and shadowy hierophants stood attentive. They were girt in leopards' skins and wore sabre-shaped teeth suspended by a string round their necks. Others had ornaments of uncut amber, or hatchets of jade threaded as collars on a cord of sinew. A few flaunted torques of gold as armlets and necklets and wore pointed hats.

The High Priest rose slowly and held out his two hands, just level with his head, the palms turned outward as he demanded, in a mystic tongue, if Yolande and Hedda had a willing human sacrifice. The two whores told him they had brought a willing victim.

The High Priest gazed at me. His glance was piercing. I trembled less with fear than with a sense of strangeness, such as a neophyte might feel on being first presented at some courtly pageant. I was conscious of some immemorial ritual. Ancestral memories seemed to stir within me, memories of the swamp.

The priest told me he wanted to conduct a ritual. It had been the rite of those who built from the days of Lokmariaker and Avebury. Every building required human souls to guard and protect it. One victim slain beneath the foundation stone became the guardian spirit against earthquake and ruin. One victim slain when the building was half up became the guardian against battle and tempest. One victim who flung herself of her own free will off tower or gable when the building was complete became the guardian against thunder and lightning. My life was required on that score.

I was dimly aware that those who offer themselves as victims for service must offer themselves willingly, for the gods demand a voluntary victim. I would be the guardian of the tower against thunder and lightning. I flung my arms round Hedda's neck. The serene peace in her strange eyes made me mysteriously in love with her and with the fate she offered me. Her eyes revolved uncannily like the stars in their orbits. Yolande unwound my arms with a gentle forbearance. She coaxed me as one coaxes an unwilling child. She held out her arms with an enticing gesture.

I sprang into Yolande's arms, sobbing in an excess of hysterical fervour. They were the arms of Death and I embraced them. Her lips were the lips of Death and I kissed them. Yolande, Yolande, I would have done anything she asked me. The tall dark girl in the simple black robe stooped down and kissed me twice on the forehead in return. Then she looked at the High Priest. From the recesses of the secret temple, from the inmost shrines of the shrouded cavern, unearthly music began to sound of itself, with wild modulation, on strange reeds and tabors.

The music swept through the aisles like a rushing wind on an Aolian harp. At times it wailed with a voice like a woman's. At times it rose loud in an organ-note of triumph. At times it sank low into a pensive and melancholy flute-like symphony. It waxed and waned. It swelled and died away again, but no man saw how or whence it proceeded. Wizard echoes issued from the crannies and vents in the invisible walls. They sighed from the ghostly interstices of the pillars. They keened and moaned from the vast overhanging dome of the palace.

Gradually the song shaped itself by weird stages into a processional measure. At its sound the High Priest rose slowly from his immemorial seat on the mighty cromlech which formed his throne. The Shades in leopards' skins ranged themselves in bodiless rows on either hand. The ghostly wearers of the sabre-toothed lions' fangs followed like ministrants in the footsteps of their hierarch. Hedda and Yolande took their places in the procession. I stood between the two, with hair floating on the air. I looked like a novice turning her first trick, accompanied and cheered by a couple of pimps.

My ghostly pageant moved off. Unworldly music followed us with fitful gusts of melody. We passed down the main corridor, between shadowy Doric pillars which grew dimmer and ever dimmer again in the distance as we approached, with slow steps, the earthward portal. At the gate, the High Priest pushed against the valves with his hand. They opened outward. He passed into the moonlight. The attendants thronged after him. As each wild figure crossed the threshold, the same strange sight as before met my eyes. For a second of time each ghostly body became luminous, as with some curious phosphorescence.

As I reached the outer air I gasped. Its freshness

almost choked me. I was conscious now that the atmosphere of the vault, though pleasant in its way, and warm and dry, had been loaded with fumes as of burning incense, and with somnolent vapours of poppy and mandragora. Its drowsy ether had cast me into a lethargy. But after the first minute in the outer world, the keen night air revived me. The procession made its way across the churchyard towards the looming tower. As we wound among the graves an owl hooted. It was the owl of Minerva.

When we passed in front of the porch, with its ancient yew-tree, a stealthy figure glided out like a ghost from the darkling shadow. It was a woman, bent and bowed, with quivering limbs. I recognised the old whore immediately. She put herself at the head of our procession. We moved on to the tower. The old harlot drew a rusty key from her pocket, and fitted it with a twist into the new lock. When she looked round grinning, I shrank from her, but I followed on still into the ringers' room at the base of the tower.

A staircase led up to the summit. The High Priest mounted the stair, chanting a mystic refrain whose runic sounds were no longer intelligible to me. As I'd reached the outer air, the tongue of the dead seemed to have become a mere blank of mingled odours and murmurs to me. It was like a summer breeze, sighing through warm and resinous woods. But Yolande and Hedda spoke to me yet, to cheer me, in the English language. I recognised that as revenants they were still in touch with the upper air and the world of the disembodied bourgeois subject.

They tempted me up the stair with encouraging fingers. I followed them with confidence. The staircase was dim, but a supernatural light seemed to fill the tower, diffused from the bodies or souls of its occupants. At the head of all, the High Priest still chanted his unearthly litany in E flat. Magic sounds of chimes seemed to swim in unison with his tune as we mounted. Were those floating notes material or spiritual? We passed the belfry, no tongue of metal wagged, but the rims of the great bells resounded and reverberated to the ghostly symphony with eldritch melody.

Still we passed on and upward. We reached a ladder that gave access to the final storey. Dust and cobwebs clung to it. Once more I drew back. It was dark overhead and the luminous haze began to fail. My companions still held my hands with the same kindly, persuasive touch as ever. A sweet voice encouraged me gently. It was like heavenly music. I knew not why I should consent, but nonetheless I submitted. Some spell seemed cast over me. With tremulous feet, scarcely realising what I did, I mounted the ladder and went up four steps of it.

I turned and looked down again. The old whore's wrinkled face met my frightened eyes. It was smiling horribly. I shrank back once more, terrified. The High Priest had, with his ghostly fingers, by this time opened the trap-door that gave access to the summit. A ray of moonlight slanted through the aperture. The breeze blew down with it. Once more I felt the stimulating and reviving effect of fresh air. Vivified by its chill, I struggled up to the top, passed through the trap, and found myself standing on the open platform at the summit of the tower.

The moonlight on the snow shone pale green and mysterious. For miles and miles around I could just make out, by its aid, the dim contours of the city with its thin white mantle in the solemn silence. Tower block behind tower block rose faintly shimmering. The chant had ceased, the High Priest and his acolytes were mixing strange herbs in a mazar-bowl or chalice. Stray perfumes of myrrh and of cardamoms were wafted towards me. The women in leopard skins burnt smouldering sticks of spikenard. Then Yolande led me forward, placing me close up to the white parapet.

Stone heads of virgins smiled on me. Yolande turned her face towards the east. She parted her lips and spoke in a solemn voice. I stepped by the aid of a wooden footstool onto the parapet. There, in my black weeds, with my arms spread abroad and my hair flying free, I paused for a second, as if about to shake out some wings and throw myself into the air like a swift or a swallow. I stretched my arms wider, and leaned forward as if to leap into the void. Another second and my sacrifice would have been accomplished.

But before I could launch myself from the tower, I felt a force laid upon me. I knew at once it was a restraint conjured up by my occult pimp, not that of a guardian spirit. The force of addiction lay heavy upon me. It clogged and burdened me with the drive for greater profit. With a violent effort I strove to shake myself free, and carry out my now fixed intention of self-immolation from the heights of the tower. But the force was too strong for me. I could not shake it off. It gripped and held me.

I yielded and, reeling, fell back with a gasp onto the platform of the tower. At the same moment a commotion seized the assembled spirits. A weird cry rang voiceless through the shadowy company. I heard it as if in a dream, very dim and distant. It was thin as a bat's note, almost inaudible to the ear, yet perceived by the brain or at least by the spirit. It was a cry of alarm, fright and warning. With one accord, all the host of phantoms rushed hurriedly forward to the battlements and pinnacles. The High Priest led the way.

It was a reckless rout. The spirits flung themselves from the top, like lemmings from a cliff, and floated fast through the air on invisible pinions. Hedda and Yolande, ambassadresses and intermediaries with the upper air, were the last to fly from the living presence of my crack addiction. They clasped my hand silently and looked deep into my eyes. The horde of spirits floated away on the air, as in a witches' Sabbath, to the vault whence it issued. The doors swung on their rusty hinges, and closed behind them. I wrestled alone with the force that held me.

The shock of this intervention and the sudden departure of the ghostly band in such wild disarray, threw me for a while into a state of semi-consciousness. My head reeled. My brain swam. I clutched for support at the parapet of the tower. But the force that held me sustained me still. I felt myself gently drawn down with quiet mastery and lay on a stone tomb close by the tower. I clutched the money I'd taken from a john, while he puffed and panted on top of me. His breath was warm and foul against the night air.

When he reached orgasm, the taxi driver who was fucking me collapsed momentarily. His weight pressed me down and I could feel the sepulchre I was spread across pressing coldly against my back. When he got up, I eased myself from the tomb. Several members of the International Communist Current were prising open a neighbouring vault. The mausoleum door gave way and the militants pulled out George Lansbury's coffin. Though more than fifty years had passed since his funeral, the Labour hack's features were tinted with the warmth of life. His eyes open. No cadaverous odour exhaled from the coffin.

There was faint but appreciable respiration and corresponding action of the heart. The limbs were still flexible, the flesh elastic. The body lay immersed in blood. This was surely proof of vampirism. The body was raised and a sharp stake driven through its heart. At that moment it uttered a piercing shriek, in all respects such as might escape from a living person in the last agony. Then the head was struck off and a torrent of blood flowed from the severed neck. The body and head were next placed on a pile of wood, and burned away to ashes.

Presently the militants were approached by a tall, slim man with rich black hair and ethereal features. He was the sort of bloke who might be overlooked on a dance floor, but in the moonlight I could see he possessed a beauty that went beyond your obvious pink-and-white prettiness. His eyes, in particular, had a lustrous depth that was almost superhuman, and his fingers and nails were strangely transparent in their waxen softness. A shout went up from the assembled activists. Not daring to confront JJ the zombie master in a graveyard, they ran. JJ turned towards me.

As I stood, motionless, meeting his glance without the twitching of an eyebrow or the tremor of a hand, I saw that he began to consider me even more intently. And perhaps it was the peculiarity – to say the least of it – of my appearance that caused him to suspect that he was face to face with an adventure of particular attractiveness to a top-flight zombie master. Whether he took me for an adept I cannot say, but from his manner I think it possible he did. He began to move towards me, addressing me with the utmost courtesy.

I made no attempt to stare him out. Even supposing that he utilized those hypnotic powers with which nature had to a dangerous degree endowed him to force me to have sex with him, there was little to fear: I was, after all, a prostitute, and he was very good looking. As far as I was concerned, a zombie master's money was as good as a taxi driver's. JJ read my thoughts. He told me he wasn't interested in sex, but that it had been a very long time since some of his zombies had last got their end away.

I nearly fainted when I saw the size of the first zombie's donger. It was huge, and behind this John Holmes clone stretched a long line of equally well-endowed members of the living dead. It seemed that JJ was particularly keen on using zombified male porn stars to achieve his self-imposed task of turning prole-tarians away from the party spirit and towards the circle spirit. However, wetting my knickers turned out to be a futile waste of bodily fluids. The zombie began playing with himself in an attempt to get an erection and his undead dick dropped off.

Once the distraught zombie master and his minions had dispersed, my next john was John Gray. He was exceptionally tall and thin. His limbs were exceedingly long and emaciated. His forehead was broad and low. His complexion was absolutely bloodless. His mouth was large and flexible, and his teeth were more wildly uneven, although apparently sound, than I had ever before seen teeth in a human head. The expression of his smile, however, was by no means unappealing, as might be supposed – but it had no variation whatever. It was one of profound melancholy – of a phaseless and unceasing gloom.

Gray's temperament was insensitive and unenthusiastic. His imagination was singularly dull and uncreative, and derived additional lassitude from his habitual use of morphine, without which he found it impossible to exist. Like most junkies, Gray was not particularly interested in sex. He would pay prostitutes to walk abroad with him until he became excited enough to consummate that which he invariably had to pay for in advance. I bent my steps immediately to his. The cemetery was beginning to empty itself of prostitutes and johns, and had about it an indescribable and, to me, a delicious, aspect of dreary desolation.

The solitude seemed absolutely virginal. I could not help imagining that the gravel path upon which we trod had never before been trodden by the feet of human beings. The thick and peculiar mist which hung heavily over the graveyard served, no doubt, to deepen the vague impressions which the tombs created. So dense was this pleasant fog that I could at no time see more than a dozen yards of the path before me. This path was excessively sinuous, and as the moon could not be seen, I soon lost all sense of the direction in which I journeyed.

There came a whole universe of suggestion – a gay and motley train of rhapsodical and immethodical thought. As I busied myself in this, we walked on. The mist deepened around us to so great an extent that at length we were reduced to a clumsy groping of the way. An indescribable uneasiness took hold of me without warning – a species of nervous hesitation and tremor. I feared to tread, lest I should be precipitated unwittingly into some abyss. I remembered, too, strange stories told about graveyards. A thousand vague fancies oppressed and disconcerted me – fancies the more distressing because vague.

To dream of teeth drawn means loss of friends. To dream of music signifies speedy marriage. To dream of falling out denotes constancy. To dream of a ring falling off your finger signifies the loss of a friend. To dream of a coffin signifies the death of a friend. To dream of birds singing signifies joy. To fight with and destroy serpents denotes victory over enemies. To dream of kisses denotes love from a friend. To fly high signifies praise. To be at a feast and eat greedily signifies sickness. To dream of sex indicates lust. Dream on, my friends.

Very suddenly my attention was arrested by the loud beating of a drum. My amazement was, of course, extreme, until a new and still more astounding source of interest and perplexity arose. There came a wild rattling or jingling sound, as if of a bunch of large keys, and upon the instant a half-naked man rushed past us with a shriek. He came so close to us that I felt his hot breath upon my cold face. He bore in one hand an instrument composed of an assemblage of steel rings, and shook them extremely vigorously as he ran.

Scarcely had he disappeared in the fog before, panting after him, with open mouth and glaring eyes, there darted a huge zombie. The sight of this monster rather relieved than heightened my terrors – for JJ had promised that I would come to no harm in the graveyard since it was not my fault if the legions of the undead suffered from impotency and dick rot. I stepped boldly and briskly forward. At length, quite overcome by exertion, and by a certain oppressive closeness of the atmosphere, we seated ourselves on a tomb. Presently there came a feeble gleam of moonlight.

Silver spots boiled in front of my eyes, it was the most disgusting thing I ever lay down for. All over me like a cheap suit. Words foaming, clothes foaming, break out of grey death. Repossessed the child's cyber pet and evicted the family from their cardboard box in the Charing Cross Road. Gray didn't care, Gray hadn't been invaded by the Big Ugly Spirit, he was the Big Ugly Spirit. No good. *No bueno.* Six foot under, broadcasting live from the last promenade of the centuries. Rich bastards always complain because their money only buys sex and not love.

John Gray arose hurriedly and in a state of fearful agitation ran from me screaming. A figure emerged from the fog and struck me upon the right temple with a blunt instrument. I reeled and fell. An instantaneous and dreadful sickness seized me. I struggled – I gasped – I died. For many minutes my sole feeling was that of darkness and nonentity, with the consciousness of death. At length there seemed to pass a violent and sudden shock through my soul, as if of electricity. With it came a sense of elasticity and of light. This latter I felt – not saw.

A steward announced that the couple walking back to their seats had just made love in the toilet and requested a round of applause. Frightened some kiddies, others found the words incomprehensible. The tabloids offered money to readers for names of sexy bitch twenty-nine (me) and boyfriend thirty-one.

Several requests that the security camera footage be screened on the in-flight movie system for the amusement of business flyers – but the captain wanted the video for his private collection and wasn't prepared to share without hefty payment. No one onboard was willing to cough up enough green stuff.

In an instant I seemed to rise from the ground. But I had no bodily, no visible, audible, or palpable presence. Beneath me lay my corpse, the whole head greatly swollen and disfigured. But all these things I felt – not saw. I took interest in nothing. Even the corpse seemed a matter in which I was unconcerned. Volition I had none, yet appeared to be impelled into motion, and flitted buoyantly out of the graveyard, retracing the circuitous route by which I had entered it. Along faceless streets I fled, impelled to follow them against my will and better judgement.

When I had attained that street in Shadwell at which I had encountered my occult pimp and passed several nights, I again experienced a shock as of a galvanic battery, the sense of weight, of volition, of substance, returned. I became my original self, and bent my steps eagerly homeward – not to the pimp's house, but back to the cemetery, for that was now my home. I belonged among the moss-laden graves and amid the sweet smell of death. This was my origin as well as my destiny. The popular imagination connects prostitution to death – both socially and literally.

The main reason I took up prostitution as an art form was that I once did a series of performances in which a computer-aided machine was programmed to take random quantities of my blood, including potentially life-threatening measures. I established a blood bank of my own body fluids to archive what I'd planned to be my life's work. Unfortunately, a ghoul broke into the blood bank and drank several pints, then in a fit of madness committed a vampiric attack on a twenty year old camper in the Lake District. I took to crack and prostitution in pique.

The rosy fingers of dawn were breaking across the grey cityscape. I made my way into a vandalised crypt and lay down on a coffin. When I awoke, it was dark, and there was an ornately worked Celtic bronze ring on my marriage finger that I couldn't recall having seen before. However, it wasn't the fading shine in the curious metal ring which daunted my eye and quickened with terror the pulse of my fast-beating heart. The buildings beyond the graveyard were on fire. From the background of the city rose roaring flames, half-smothered in dense, black smoke.

I beheld the dread conflagration. The fire was advancing – wave upon wave, clear and red as the rush of a flood through the mists of some lightning-crowned mountain peak. Roused from my stupor at the first sight of danger, I sat up and watched the advancing destruction through the broken windows of the crypt. I'd ceased to care who or what my tempter was, focusing instead on turning profitable tricks. Clouds had gathered over the sky, and though the moon gleamed at times in the gaps that they left in the blue air, her beam was hazy and dulled.

Then I watched the final dawn break, I could see that the sun was hugely greater than it had been the last time I'd seen it. So great was it, that its lower edge touched the far horizon as the top rose high above me. Even as I watched, I imagined that it drew closer. The radiance of green that lit the earth grew steadily brighter and brighter. Thus, for a long space, were things. Then, on a sudden, I saw that the sun was changing shape and growing smaller, just as the moon would have done in past time.

After a while, only a third of the illuminated part of the sun was turned towards the earth. A star bore away on the left. Gradually, as the world moved on, the star shone upon the front of the crypt where I lay hidden from the cares of our decayed and dying world. The sun showed only as a great bow of green fire. An instant, it seemed, and the sun had vanished completely. The star was still fully visible. Then the earth moved into the black shadow of the sun, and all was night. Night: black, starless, and intolerable.

Filled with tumultuous thoughts, I watched across the night – waiting. Years, it may have been. Then, in the darkness about me, the clotted stillness of the world was broken. I seemed to hear a soft padding of many feet, and a faint, inarticulate whisper of sound. I looked abut me into the blackness and saw a multitude of eyes. As I stared, they increased, and appeared to come towards me. For an instant, I stood, unable to move. Then a hideous noise rose up into the night, and at that I leapt from the crypt out into the frozen world.

I have a confused notion of having run for a while. After that, I just waited and waited. Several times I heard shrieks, always as though from a distance. Aside for these sounds, I had no idea of the whereabouts of the graveyard. Time moved onward. I was conscious of little, save for sensations of cold and hopelessness and fear. An age, it seemed, and there came a glow that told of the coming light. It grew tardily. Then – with a loom of unearthly glory – the first ray from a green star struck over the edge of the dark sun.

The ray lit the world and fell upon a ruined stone structure, some hundred yards away. The world moved out into the light of the star and it seemed to stretch across a quarter of the heavens. The glory of its livid light was so tremendous that it appeared to fill the sky with quivering flames. Then I saw the sun. It was so close that half of its diameter lay below the horizon and, as the world circled across its face, it seemed to tower right up into the sky, a stupendous dome of emerald coloured fire and flame.

I took shelter from the chill wind in the grim ruin. Years seemed to pass, slowly. The earth had almost reached the centre of the sun's disk. The light from the green sun – as it must now be called – shone through the interstices that gapped the mouldered walls about me, giving them the appearance of being wrapped in green flames. Suddenly there rose a loud roar, and up from the centre of a roofless building shot a vast column of blood-red flame. I saw the little, twisted towers and turrets flash into fire, yet still preserving their twisted crookedness.

The beams of the green sun beat down upon the building and intermingled with its lurid glows, so that it appeared as a blazing furnace of red and green fire. I watched, mesmerised, until an overwhelming sense of approaching danger drew my attention. I glanced up and the sun was closer. So close, in fact, that it seemed to overhang the world. The huge bulk of the sun rose high above me. The distance between it and the earth diminished rapidly. Then, suddenly, the earth shot forward. In a moment it had traversed the space between it and the sun.

It seemed to leap almost to the distant green sun – shearing through the emerald light, a very cataract of blinding fire. It reached its limit and sank, and on the sun glowed a vast splash of burning white – the grave of the earth. The sun was very close to me now. The green sun was now so huge that its breadth seemed to fill up all the sky ahead. A year may have gone by – or, indeed, several unrecorded, unlamented centuries. Aeons of eternity enveloped me but it was still too fleetingly tht the world was becalmed with unearthly silence.

The sun showed far in front – a black circular mass against the molten splendour of the great green orb. Near one edge, I observed that a lurid glow had appeared, marking the place where the moon had fallen into it. By this I knew that the long-dead sun was still revolving, though with terrible slowness. I could hear cries, strange inhuman cries, and sounds like the crunching of glass under marching feet. The world turned. London was no longer even a ruin. It had disappeared from the face of eternity and the cosmos. I longed for death or sleep.

Far to my right, I seemed at moments to catch a faint glow of whitish light. For a long time I was uncertain whether to put this down to fancy or not. Thus, for a while, I stared with fresh wonderings, until at last I knew that it was no imaginary thing but a reality. It grew brighter, and presently there slid out of the green a pale globe of softest white. It came nearer and I saw that it was apparently surrounded by a robe of gently glowing clouds. Time passed so slowly. Time passed so very, very slowly.

I longed for release and shut my eyes, but the shadow play continued much as before. I turned my face. Fell down on my back. My eye lids flickered open. I glanced towards the diminishing sun. It showed only as a dark blot on the face of the green sun. As I watched I saw it grow smaller, steadily, as though rushing towards the superior orb at an immense speed. With this turn, my interest was fully engaged. Intently, I stared. What would happen? I was conscious of extraordinary emotions as I realised that it would strike the green sun.

It grew no bigger than a pea. The earth was being pulled along behind it. I wanted to turn over and bury my head in darkness. I pushed up my hips, got part of the way there. An arm jammed underneath my body prevented me getting all the way over. I rolled onto my back, raising my arm above my head, and pushed with my hips. This time I rolled right over. I couldn't see a thing. Distant thunder, very distant thunder, slowly rolling away into silence. Yes, this is the ghetto, and the ghetto is the graveyard of ideology.

Oh. To begin. Not necessarily easy. Escape the upright men. Gender inscribes itself in crime. To become what I was not. To immerse myself in a new life. *Cum multis aliis quae nunc praescriber longum est*. With much else too long to set down here. I was determined to subvert the present with the past. The art I pursued was to set ghosts walking. I was a walking mort on Quaker Street. Are you looking for some pussy darling? A cony catcher in Brick Lane. A cross-biting bitch in Hoxton. A prigger of prancers. A counterfeit crank. Wicked walker. Dell.

### Grief by John B Spencer

'*Grief* is a speed-freak's cocktail, one part Leonard and one part
Ellroy, that goes right to the head.' George P Pelecanos
When disparate individuals collide, it's Grief.
John B Spencer's final and greatest novel.
'Spencer writes the tightest dialogue this side of Elmore Leonard,
so bring on the blood, sweat and beers!' Ian Rankin

### No One Gets Hurt by Russell James

'The best of Britain's darker crime writers' – *The Times*
After a friend's murder Kirsty Rice finds herself drawn into
the murky world of call-girls, porn and Internet sex.

### Kiss It Away by Carol Anne Davis

'Reminiscent of Ruth Rendell at her darkest' – Booklist (USA)
Steroid dependent Nick arrives alone in Salisbury, rapes a
stranger and brutally murders a woman.
'A gripping tale of skewered psychology... a mighty chiller,'
*The Guardian*

### A Man's Enemies by Bill James

'Bill James can write, and then some' *The Guardian*
The direct sequel to 'Split'. Simon Abelard, the section's 'token
black', has to dissuade Horton from publishing his memoirs.

### End of the Line by K T McCaffrey

'KT McCaffrey is an Irish writer to watch' RTE
Emma is celebrating her Journalist of the Year Award when she
hears of the death of priest Father Jack O'Gorman in what
appears to have been a tragic road accident.

### Vixen by Ken Bruen

'Ireland's version of Scotland's Ian Rankin' – *Publisher's Weekly*
BRANT IS BACK! If the Squad survives this incendiary
installment, they'll do so with barely a cop left standing.

### The Justice Factory by Paul Charles

'If you like Morse you'll love Kennedy' – *Talking Music*, BBC
Radio 2.
'Paul Charles is one of the hidden treasures of British crime
fiction.' – John Connolly

### Ike Turner – King of Rhythm by John Collis

At last, respected rock and blues writer John Collis has written the first major study of one of music's most complex characters.

### A Dysfunctional Success – The Wreckless Eric Manual by Eric Goulden

'A national treasure' – Jonathan Ross
Wreckless Eric first found fame in the 1970s when he signed to the emergent Stiff Records. His label-mates included Ian Dury, Elvis Costello and Nick Lowe.
'Much more than a biography, *A Dysfunctional Success* is very possibly the most entertaining read this or any other year.'
– *Mojo*

## Judas Pig by 'Horace Silver'

Billy Abrahams is a career criminal who makes a very good living from violence, armed robbery, operating sex shops and stealing from other criminals. But he becomes increasingly haunted by childhood ghosts and by the ever-growing influence of Danny, his psychopathic partner in crime.

Billy finds himself starting to look beyond the violence and the scams, slowly descending into a drug-fuelled netherworld that affects his judgment and his perceptions. He is finally tipped over the edge when Danny commits an act even Billy cannot stomach. And that's when things really start to go wrong...

Judas Pig is the real deal. This explosive first novel from a reformed career criminal comes with authenticity stamped all the way through. Dark and vivid, bleak yet often funny and beautifully written, this is a book that will stay with you long after you turn the final page.

## Confessions of a Romantic Pornographer by Maxim Jakubowski

Following the death of a minor league writer, a mysterious woman whose own past is full of contradictions is called in to investigate his life and to discover the lost manuscript of his memoirs, lest they incriminate people in high places.

Her journey of discovery becomes a dazzling and confusing exploration of the nature of autobiography and the awfully grey zones between truth and fiction. With every new revelation come another series of questions.

# The Do-Not Press
## Fiercely Independent
## Publishing

## www.thedonotpress.com

All our books are available in good bookshops or
– in the event of difficulty – direct from us:
The Do-Not Press Ltd, Dept D&O,
16 The Woodlands
London
SE13 6TY
(UK)

If you do not have Internet access you can write
to us at the above address in order to join our
mailing list and receive fairly regular news on
new books and offers. Please mark your card 'No
Internet' or 'Luddite'.